Desolation

By

Lillie Carr

This novel is a work of fiction. It contains explicit material. Parental advisory. INTENDED FOR A MATURE AUDIENCE. Any reference to real people, events, establishments, organizations, or locales are intended only to give the fiction a sense of reality and authenticity. Other names, characters, and incidents are either the product of the author's imagination or are used fictitiously, as are those fictionalized events and incidents that involve real persons.

Cover Design by Lillie Carr

ISBN-13: 978-0692999363

ISBN-10: 0692999361

Printed in the United States of America

Desolation

"What do we have here?" Samuel Stone, the lead FBI agent, asked Thomas, the lead detective.

"A crime scene from Hell," replied Thomas.

It was not just any regular crime scene. The bodies were everywhere in pieces. Every corner of the room was stacked at least three feet high with multiple body parts. FBI agents, veteran policeman, and detectives were leaving the hotel room to vomit at random. The killer or killers are the most sadistic masochist killers that have ever existed in history on a serial killer level. No remorse, no set pattern and no clues were left to enable the FBI agents and detectives to begin to have a lead. They covered their tracks thoroughly.

"It's going to be a long night," said the Coroner. "It looks like it's over thirty bodies here. I've counted thirty-two heads so far," she said. "And that's just two corners of this four corner room."

Samuel gasps and stops breathing for a few seconds. All he could think of is that it is happening again, but how could that be? He was a child at the age of three when his father, a detective, was working on the gruesome murder cases. Now thirty-two years later, the same MO. Even more strange is that the same type of killings happened thirty-two years before the last one when he was three years old. However, this time it is different. This is the third crime scene found like this within two weeks. The last two prior timeframes of killings were single isolated incidents, no repeats. One crime scene of a total of sixty-four bodies and the killer or killers went cold turkey never to be heard from again until thirty-two years later. It is impossible to think that it is the same killer or killers. Samuel looks around the third crime scene in awe. He thought to himself, what is different? Why three mass killings verses one? Would there be a fourth one or more? How did the killer or killers get all these people in this room and kill them? My father lost a lot of sleep over trying to solve that case thirty-two years ago. I guess it is my turn now.

"There are no rhyme or reason to the layout of the bodies. The body parts are mixed up and thrown about at random," said the coroner. "It's like the killer was in a state of rage and savagely ripped the bodies apart. There was no knife or cutting object used. The amount of strength and endurance that it would take to accomplish such brutality is beyond comprehension, beyond reality, beyond human," she said.

Sarah, the coroner, let her voice get lower while speaking more slowly as she came to the end of her statement. All she could think of was what kind of savage would do this?

"I think I found the head of a child," one of the uniformed police officers said in a low voice.

"No, make that two children," he corrected his statement.

A silence came over the room. Everyone stopped what he or she was doing. Some gasped, while others stopped breathing altogether. Two vomited where they stood. After about a minute of silence that seems like a lifetime, Samuel speaks up.

"Okay everyone, let's get this bastard. Go by the book on everything. The last thing we want is to let this son of a bitch get away on a technicality."

He moves to the far left of the room while being careful not to step on any body parts.

"Do you need help in processing some of the bodies?" he asked Sarah once he made it to her side and was able to make eye contact with her.

"I welcome all the help you can give me," she replied while maintaining eye contact with him as well.

"Come sit beside me on the floor at my feet," she said to them. "Don't speak, listen to what I have to say and watch what I am going to do."

The two six-foot-plus men who are weighing over two hundred and twenty-five pounds both with shoulder length dark brown wavy hair with model-like facial features obeyed and sat on the floor one on each side of her feet.

"Come," she commanded.

A woman and a man are being led into the room by four other muscular men with dark brown shoulder length hair. The woman is resistive at first until she sees who has summoned her. She immediately becomes submissive and yields to being led into the room. Her petite body is covered by a black above the knee loose fitting dress that flows gracefully through the air as she walks towards the Mistress who has summoned her. Her short blonde hair hugs her beautiful angelic like face. Her eyes are coral blue that instantly goes from fierce to submissive when they lock onto the Mistress. The man is expressionless. He walks at the pace his captors set. His body is all muscles under his black leather vest and pants. He has short light brown hair that encases his Greek God-like facial features.

"Absolutely stunning, both of you. The things that I would do to you both if we met today under different circumstances would be nothing short of pure sadistic erotic pleasure, but you both meet me under different circumstances. I will tell you this; I will get great pleasure out of what I am going to do to you both just the same." Mistress said to them both with a sinister smile forming on her face.

"Now tell me why did you do what you did and try to hide it from me? Did you not think I would find it out? Why did you kill one of my servants?" she asked.

Mistress looks over to one of the tall, muscular men standing against the left wall and commands "Bring her in."

He leaves the room. Everyone is silent until he returns with a little girl around the age of ten. The woman gasps while the man for the first time becomes resistive to his captors. Both start to speak, but with the wave of her hand slightly, the Mistress takes away their ability to make a sound for the moment.

"This is your demon child possessing this human correct?" she asked.

The woman nods her head yes as tears form in her eyes and roll down her cheeks.

"You know my rule, a life for a life," Mistress said in a low domineering voice. "You made my servant suffer," she stated. "It's only fitting I do the same for your child."

Even though the child looks young and innocent, there is an evil demon inside of her over three hundred years old, which is a whisper in time in the demon world. Mistress is dressed in a purple form fitting dress that flares out at the hips. Her caramel colored skin with dark brown shoulder length hair and black eyes with full black woman lips make her beauty both alluring and foreboding. Her voluptuous body of curves enhanced her sexuality. All desired to touch her, taste her and feel her warmth and dominance. Her sexual desire is nothing short of insatiable. Her dominance is strikingly overpowering coupled with her beauty, which makes her irresistible. She is clearly the demon in charge of all other demons. When she was asked her name, she would only respond, "I am who I am." All called her Mistress and considered themselves her slave by choice as well as by her will.

"Stay," she commanded with a smile forming on her face to the demon child, which prohibited the demon from leaving the child's body.

There was no question that Mistress is the oldest and most powerful demon in existence. A slight smile forms over Mistress's face as she looks at the two adult demon captives. She turns her glance towards the demon child. With a slight wave of her hand, she strips the entire layer of skin off the child along with her clothes as well. The demon child screams out in agony.

"Ahh what did I do wrong?" the demon child yelled out between agonizing screams.

"You did nothing child. You are paying for the crimes of your parents." Mistress explained.

Then with the wave of her hand again, Mistress takes all the fat content off the child's body, leaving nothing but blood-tinged glittering muscles. The child demon screams out in pain.

"Stop! Take Me!" screamed the demon father once he was able to speak again.

"What fun would that be?" asked Mistress with a smirk on her face.

"Please stop! Punish us! Take our lives, not hers!" the demon mother cried out.

"It is not your lives I require at the moment, but your turn will come soon enough," Mistress taunted her.

Mistress looks at the child demon and squeezes her right fist slowly shut. As she did, the demon child's body seems to concave on itself. At first, the demon child starts to scream, but when the air is slowly squeezed out of her lungs, she cannot produce a sound. The pain and agony on her face are excruciating. Both the Father and Mother demons are yelling out for Mistress to stop. Their cries are ignored. Mistress holds her fist tightly shut until the life drains from the demon child's face and eyes. When Mistress lets her right hand relax, the child demon's body goes limp. Her captor releases her body, and it falls lifeless to the floor.

"A life for a life," Mistress said to the two adult demons forming at the mouth on the floor.

She revels in their pain, their vulnerability and their helplessness. Mistress smiles in delight.

"Now it's your turn."

"Troy I have to take care of some business today, so I am going to need you to keep an eye on the construction while I'm gone. The foreman already knows that I won't be at the worksite for the rest of the day. I will come in early tomorrow morning and inspect the work that they are doing today. Pay attention to the beams they are putting in. I know that I don't have to tell you that, but the perfectionist in me compels me to do so." Terrance said to Troy with a half chuckle.

Troy is used to Terrance anal ways. He just smiles and says "I know man. It's all good. I got things here. Do what you have to do. I know how to reach you if I have a question." Troy replied.

"Thanks, man," Terrance said as he walks over to his desk and grabs his coat.

Today is the day he will be meeting with all the other first lieutenants in the park to meet their leader for the first time face to face. He has heard so many things about her. All good of course, but he will still have to determine if she is someone he would follow. He would follow the Archangel, Michael and the other angels with no problem. He trusts them. Even though the angels say that she is the leader, trust is earned not a given privilege in his mind. Terrance walks over and gives Troy a notepad with a checklist that has to be inspected throughout the day as well as at the end of the day.

"This list is getting longer and longer man," Troy says to Terrance in half humorous and half serious voice.

"I know. That's why you get paid the big bucks." Terrance said laughing out loud as he turns and walks out the door.

"I need a raise," Troy yells as the door closes.

Terrance would have enjoyed sticking around to haggle with Troy, but today he has to be in the park to fulfill a promise to an angel.

There is an overcast today, which is not as nice as the two previous days. Auroa had an overpowering urge to go to the park today for some strange reason. It was apparently not because it was such a nice I got to be outside and basking in the sun kind of day. Of all days to want to be outside, this is the day I picked she thought to herself. The park is uncommonly crowded today. There have to be hundreds of people gathered in the middle of the park. They all appear to be together as well. Maybe it is for some big company picnic she thought. However, there is nothing cooking. The people are all different ages, economic background, and races. No uniforms or business clothes. Some were dressed inappropriately for a company function she thought as she looked at the young girl in her late teens or early twenties wearing hip-hugging shorts and a sports bra. Her flat belly is showing off the silver and gold navel ring that dangled down to the top of her low waistline hip-hugging shorts. Pretty she thought. Definitely inappropriate.

As Auroa gets closer to the center of the crowd, a man looks over at her. He looks as though he recognizes her, which is impossible because she never saw him a day in her life.

"It's time," he said when he locks his eyes on Auroa.

Without breaking his gaze on her, he steps up on a three-step stool that elevates him slightly above the crowd. While maintaining his gaze on Auroa, he starts to chant some words that were not English. At least Auroa did not understand them. As he raises his voice, a silence falls over the crowd. All are looking at him. The wind picks up. Auroa becomes alarmed, nervous and tries to exit the crowd. The crowd would not let her leave. Am I in the middle of some satanic cult she thought to herself.

"Let me through!" she cried out, but the crowd is unyielding.

They would not let her pass. The wind is slightly overpowering at times, but the crowd would not disperse. The sky becomes dark. The wind bellows while the man continues to scream out his incantations while staring at Auroa. Somehow the crowd starts to break up into small groups of about fifteen to twenty people. If she did not see it with her own eyes, not once but twice, she would not have believed it. In the middle of each small gathering of people, a man or a woman appears out of thin air wearing loose-fitting white slacks with a knee-length white coat that is opened in the front to reveal a white shirt underneath it. All of them are stunning.

"This isn't right! Stop it!" Auroa yelled out.

No one listened, especially the man still yelling out the spell. It has to be a spell. Devil worshipers thought Auroa. As she turns to run out of the crowd that has opened up to allow her to leave now, a man over six feet tall dressed in white appears before her.

"Hello Auroa," he said.

Before she could catch herself, Auroa lets out a loud scream and turns to run the other way only to have the man appear before her in that direction as well.

"Don't be afraid. I am here to protect and guide you," he said.

Startled and shaken, Auroa puts her hands on both sides of her head trying to steady herself. She feels as though she was losing her mind and touch with reality.

After a few minutes, she yells out "What is happening? What is going on?"

"My name is Michael," the man in white with dark brown thick shoulder length wavy hair with beautiful thick eyelashes and dark brown piercing eyes said to her. When he looks at Auroa, she feels as though he is looking into her soul, right down to the core of her being. Auroa wants to run again. She wants to scream. She wants to escape the insanity of this living nightmare. However, her body and mind are not connected.

All she could say is "What, how, who?"

Michael places his hand on Auroa's shoulder to steady her while looking into her eyes.

He speaks softly to her and says "Auroa my name is Michael. I am an angel. I am here to guide and protect you. You are the leader of what is to come. We have a lot of work to do."

Auroa is trying hard to still her mind. The more Michael speaks, the more it calms her while at the same time, the more he tells her spins her out of control. It is a toggle war of calm and spin out of control, sanity and insanity, stand and fall, run and stand still as well as scream and silence. All at once Auroa could stand no more. Her mind and body give way, and she falls to the ground. Michael catches her before her body hits the ground.

Michael looks at Auroa and says "Sleep, rest well. You will need it Auroa. You will earn it. You deserve it."

He picks her up and carries her out of the park. "It's time to go home Auroa," he whispered to her.

"Daisy why do you always have to see things the way that you do? Everything in life is not always about you or the end of the world if you do not get your way. Haven't I given you everything and more? I gave up my world for you because I love you, but you are killing my love with your insecurities, your lack of belief in me and you constantly telling me that I am not worth your love or that I am not making you happy. What do you want from me?" Asked Terrance in a half questioning and half pleading voice.

"Everything," replied Daisy.

"What must I do to prove my love to you?" Asked Terrance in a broken hurtful voice.

"Anything," replied Daisy.

"Daisy, I love you more than life itself, but I will not forsake my calling. I will not turn my back on what the Lord thy God has asked me to do on his behalf for the betterment of humankind. I love you Daisy, but I love God more," Terrance said to her with tears in his eyes.

Every word that came out of Terrance's mouth felt like it was cutting his chest open as it left his lips. This is the hardest thing he has ever had to do in his life. He gave up everything for Daisy. He gave up his wife, children, friends, home, dogs, some business associates and even his old church for the love that he thought he had found with Daisy. He now realizes that the more he gives her, the more she wants. She is never satisfied. Now she is asking him to choose her over God and God's will. She is not the woman he thought she was. He realizes at this very moment that she does not love him. She loves what she can get out of him. If he loses his wealth, he realizes that he would lose her too. Terrance leans forward while still sitting on the couch. He buries his face in both of his hands. His heart is heavy and breaking every second he sits there in silence while she waits for his answer. Finally, he lifts his face out of his hands to reveal the tears of a broken man. He takes a deep breath while standing slowly. He feels resolved.

"Goodbye, Daisy. I love you, but not more than God. I need and love him more than I do you. Goodbye." he said as he walks past her to leave the room.

"Goodbye? Are you leaving me? What do you mean goodbye? I thought you loved me!" she screams out in disbelief like a spoiled child who is not getting her most wanted toy for Christmas.

"I love God more. Goodbye," replied Terrance in a broken voice as he continued to walk across the room towards the front door of their newly renovated high rise ocean view condo.

"If you leave, don't bother coming back! This would be my home! All of it would be mine!" Daisy screamed out the ultimatum to his back.

"You can have it all Daisy. I won't be back, and I won't take care of you or your needs anymore. This home and its contents are my final gifts to you." Terrance said as he made it to the steps leading up to the massive foyer before the front door.

"You will regret this!" She screams out.

Terrance did not reply as he closes the door slowly behind him as if he is closing a poorly written chapter in his life. Yes, he has regrets, but not the ones that she thinks he has. He regrets all the parts of his life that were Daisy. Yes, WERE is the keyword. She is past tense. He is no longer looking at her. He is definitely looking past her for the first time in the six years that they have been together. The more steps he takes away from her, the better he feels and breathes. I am walking from hell to God, from darkness to light, from being used to being useful, from hostility to tranquility and from being condemned to salvation. Yes definitely looking past her thought Terrance as he drives off in his black Mercedes Benz while manually shifting the gear with hope for not only for the future of humankind but hope for his salvation as well.

Samuel was astonished at the coroner's report. He had never seen anything like this in all his years with the Bureau. There have been only two FBI cases in the past years long ago that is exactly like the recent murder scenes. Sixty-four bodies of men, women, and children of different backgrounds and ethnic groups were found in the room. The bodies had been ripped apart. No cutting tool was used. All of the victims were alive while being torn apart, which resulted in their deaths. No one heard screams. No one saw the people enter the building, yet along the room. Not all the victims have been identified. However, the ones that are identified are from a total of thirty-six states across the country. How was this possible?

This has been a very sad nerve gripping and gut-wrenching past three days Samuel thought to himself. All of the old detectives of the past old cases, except for two, are dead who worked on the similar case thirty-two years ago. One has dementia, which is no help to Samuel and the other is on a plane heading to meet Samuel at this very moment. Samuel has so many questions for the retired veteran detective Jones. Hopefully, he can fill in the blanks and shed some light on the case that has so many dark places.

"Agent Stone this case just keeps getting more and more bizarre. Ten of the victims are from the Catholic churches on 23rd Street and 42nd Street. There are two priest and eight nuns among the victims," said Thomas. Samuel's body goes limp, and he falls back into his chair with a mind-boggling look on his face. That hits home. Samuel was an altar boy at the 23rd Street Catholic church when he was a young boy. Hopefully, it is not Father Hanningan.

"Who are the priests?" Samuel asked.

"A Father Tonelli and Father Spetini," replied Thomas.

Samuel lets out a breath of relief. Thank God it is not Father Hannigan he thought to himself. He was like a second father to

Samuel. He made the church feel like his home away from home. He is one of Samuel's closest friends and confident as well as spiritual advisor. Samuel has a feeling that he will be seeing the Father very soon for some much-needed guidance on what he thinks will be his darkest days to come.

Tonight is beautiful out with a breeze thought Karen as she walks along the sidewalk that lines the small mom and pop shops and old stores. The section of the town she is in is all but deserted due to the new strip malls that seemed to have sprung up into being overnight ten minutes away. Even the cars took an alternate route to the neighborhoods that were close by. Karen just happens to be in need of a book that she could not find anywhere else.

"I guess the new stores do not have everything," she told the store clerk when she visited the new bookstore in the strip mall a couple of days ago.

She was bound and determined to find the book by her favorite author. She had all the other books that he had written and needed just one more to complete her collection. Karen did not realize how far she had parked her car away from the store.

"Karen," she said to herself in an annoyed voice. She decides to go back to her car instead of going to another bookstore that is about a block and a half in the other direction. As she starts to walk towards her car, she had a very foreboding feeling come across her. The wind begins to pick up. Karen instinctively picks up her pace of walking. As she did, she hears footsteps close behind her. Maybe someone came out of one of the stores she passed she thought to herself. As she quickens her footsteps, so does the person behind her. Karen begins to get nervous. She has to turn around to see who is there as well as to see how close the person is to her. To her surprise, there is no one there when she turned around to look. The footsteps stopped as well. When Karen turns back to face the direction towards her car, a man is about a foot in front of her. She gasps for air as she stops abruptly. Her heart is racing. She feels like she is about to pass out.

"You, you, you scared me," she managed to say while gasping for air.

The man just smiles in a way that scares Karen even more. Before she could say anything, the man raises up a hand with long fingernails and slashes Karen across the face. The blow takes off the entire left side of her face. Karen falls lifeless to the pavement. She is the first demon kill of the night. Mistress will be pleased. The man disappears as quickly as he appeared leaving Karen's lifeless body on the pavement to be found by a soon to be local out for a nightly jog.

Samuel hates driving to the airport. The traffic and craziness of outgoing and incoming passengers always seem chaotic to him. However, today he has to do what he has to do. No one else is available to pick up the retired old detective from the airport today. These murders, as well as other crimes on the streets, have everyone tied up. Damn yellow cab thought Samuel as one of them cut him off by pulling out in front of him without warning before he pulls into the line for the parking garage. If he had not slammed on his breaks, he would have hit the cab on the right side midway the vehicle. Again it makes Samuel think about how much he hates driving to and from the airport.

The ticket guy for the garage looks at Samuel intently while strangely holding his stare as Samuel grabs the parking ticket and throws it on his dashboard. It makes Samuel look one more time at the ticket issuer. Yes, it is weird how he is still staring at Samuel. If he didn't know better, he could swear the guy is oddly smirking at him, which he had no reason to do so. Samuel drives up three levels in the garage before finding a parking space, which he did not want to take. The space is going to be a tight fit between two large SUVs. However, he may not find another one anytime soon, so he decided to take a chance on that the doors of his car may or may not get dinged by either vehicle. A very tight fit thought Samuel as he gets out of the car and makes a great effort not to hit the SUV with his door. The garage is quiet and empty except for occasional vehicles coming up the ramp passing by him heading to the next level to find a possible parking space. With all the hustle and bustle of inbound and outbound flight as well as pickups and drop-offs, one would think that there would be the hustle and bustle of people in the parking garage as well. No that is not the case thought Samuel as he makes it to the sliding opening doors of the inner airport, which reveal the chaos of travelers going to different places within the airport.

Flight 326 United at 6 pm showed that it arrived ten minutes ago. Samuel proceeds to the baggage claim area. As he was walking to the baggage conveyor, Samuel recognizes the old detective from a picture on his DMV record. Also, Samuel notices something strange as well. Two huge men are standing about fifteen feet behind him, just looking at him. The two men are very handsome, which strikes Samuel as odd that he would think that. They do not fit in with what they are doing. They are not talking to each other, not looking around for someone in the airport or looking for a direction to go to in the airport. They are not looking at the conveyor for their luggage. They are only looking at Mr. Jones. Samuel walks over to Mr. Jones and introduces himself. Jones looks a lot older than he is. He looks like he has weathered many storms.

"How was your flight?" Samuel asked while keeping an eye on the two men staring in their direction.

"Long," Jones replied. "I hate flying, but I know how important this matter is and time is of the essence. Otherwise, I would have driven," He said to Samuel with a sincere smile.

"Thank you for flying. I really do appreciate you dropping everything and coming out here on a minute notice," said Samuel.

"It's my pleasure. I'm retired remember. I have absolutely nothing to do. I need the excitement more than you know," Jones said laughing.

Jones reaches on the conveyor and pulls off a black suitcase trimmed in purple. It has a red ribbon tied around it.

"My wife's idea of easy identification," he explains to Samuel while pointing at the ribbon.

They both laugh out loud. As they walk away from the conveyor, Samuel notices that the two large men follow them as well. So Samuel decides to walk towards the security guard station. He shows the security guards his FBI badge and informs them that the two large men are acting strangely. He did it in a way not to alarm Jones that they were watching him. Security detains the two men while Samuel walks to his car with Jones. Security will have them for a while Samuel thought to himself. He will call later to find out what was said and what was their purpose in the airport.

The drive to the hotel near the FBI station is long, but Jones has a lot to tell Samuel. He tells Samuel about what he has been doing since retiring, his grandchildren, vacation trips to various places and his bored out of his mind lifestyle. Jones is very entertaining and funny with his Irish accent. Samuel likes him right away. Jones checks into the hotel. He puts his bags in his room and is now ready to get started right away with Samuel. He is sitting back in the car with Samuel in less than thirty minutes after leaving the car to check into his hotel. It is like he still knows how to do a lot in a small amount of time even though his life now has no time crunches at all from day to day. Samuel is impressed especially since the area they parked in takes ten minutes to walk to the hotel there and ten minutes back.

Once they got to the station, Samuel walks Jones around the office introducing him to the team. A sense of pride is noted not only in Jones but the team as well. Also, it reinforces to the agents that yes there is a silver lining. One day they will be retired as well. After all the introduction and small talk, Samuel takes Jones to a large room that has crime scene photos of all the killings in the appropriate timeline section on the wall. Jones enters the room, and instantly a solemn look comes across his face. The reality and memory of the past hit him all at once. The sleepless nights, the pressure and the families' grief are brought all back to life. One glance was all it took to take him back in time. He is in yesteryear as if it is today. Jones feels his mouth go instantly dry. His stomach becomes tight. He automatically clinches his fist when he looks at the portion of the wall that is his time frame of cases. Jones has had so many nightmares since he started his retirement. At first, the nightmare would come once every two to three months. Now lately they have been occurring at least once a month. Maybe it is a prelude to him coming back here to talk about the case. Maybe it needs to be fresh in his mind again so he could be as helpful as he could be to this nice well put together attention to detail FBI agent. Maybe he needs to do his part to help shine some light on a very dark eerie place in the past that would help them in the present as well as the future. That's a lot of maybes Jones thought to himself, a lot. If a lot is what it takes, then a lot he would do Jones thought as he takes a deep breath and relaxes his closed tight fists at his sides. He clears his throat before speaking, which does not help to keep his voice from sounding hoarse. His mouth and throat are unusually dry.

"Can I have some water?" he asked Samuel.

"Sure, sure you can," responded Samuel while springing into action to retrieve it for him. "You can have anything you want in my power to give. After all, you are my flashlight into the past." Samuel said as he left the room to get some water.

Jones walks slowly around the long rectangle table to the side of the room that has his old case crime scene pictures on the wall. He pauses a little at the edge of the table before proceeding to the wall of photos. Old memories, old failures, and old emotions are flooding back at once. He is experiencing a full gamut of emotions. It is almost overwhelming to him, but he is determined to face it head on as he always faced things in his life. Do or die; you will not win he always used to say when he had to do or experience something difficult or challenging. However, this is the one case that he had a stalemate. He could not crack it. He could not close it. It still haunts him to this very day, very minute and very second. His do or die rule just did not cut it that time.

Jones continues to walk over to the wall. He allows his eyes to stare at the top photo on the left and move from picture to picture only after taking in all that he could take in from the current photo he is viewing. Every detail is noticed from how did they lay, how did they look to what was in the photo. Then something dawn on Jones. Sixty-four bodies are torn apart, but there is not sixty-four bodies worth of blood in the room. He darted over to the other crime scene photos of different time frames. Same thing. The amount of blood in the room is not enough to indicate that sixty-four bodies bled out in it. Some of the blood is missing. Hell of a lot of the blood is missing thought Jones. How could we all have missed that? He questioned himself silently in his head.

Samuel calls the airport security to see what was going on with the two men who were following Jones at the airport before returning with the sandwiches and drinks.

"I don't know what was going on Sir. The two men both acted like and stated that they had no memory of even coming to the airport let alone being in the airport. Finally, we contacted their next of kin and sent them both to the hospital for psyche evaluations and chemical analysis of their blood, which they consented to. I'm sure after general observation and labs, they will be released to their families. I'm sorry we could not be more help, Sir," said the security man.

"No, you were very helpful. Thank you," replied Samuel.

Samuel could not help but think for some strange and illogical reason that the two men were telling the truth. What the hell is going on here he asked himself silently as he walks to the crime scene room where Jones is waiting for him.

Samuel returns to the room with sandwiches, chips, sodas, and bottles of water. He even has two Debbie cakes for dessert. He places the food and drinks on the table. He notices Jones darting back and forth between multiple crime scene photos at a fast pace with a bewildered look on his face.

"What's going on Jones?" Samuel asked.

"The blood, the blood," Jones replied. "There is not enough for sixty-four bodies. Some of it is missing. A lot of it is missing." he explained.

Samuel walks over to the crime scene photos to see for himself.

"You're right. How did we miss that?" Samuel thinks out loud while not really asking Jones the question.

Jones answers anyway. "I don't know. We all missed it. Where did the blood go? The people were killed in the rooms they were found in. That's a lot of missing blood," Jones said in almost a whisper.

Samuel has to strain himself to hear all the words that Jones is saying. It is as if he is only talking to himself and forgot that Samuel is in the room at the end of his statement.

Samuel stands next to Jones looking perplexed at the crime scene photos on the board. How did they all miss all that missing blood he thought to himself. The coroner, the detectives, the FBI agents and himself all missed something so obvious. How did we do that he asked himself silently in his head.

"The killers must have taken the blood with them, but why?" Jones asked thinking out loud. His question was not really meant for Samuel. Both men took a moment to study the crime scenes. After coming to grip with such an important omission of a vital clue, they both sat down at the end of the table with the food and drinks.

Samuel began "Jones I'm going to record this if that's okay with you."

"Yes, by all means, go ahead. I know the drill," Jones said.

"Good. Tell me all that you remember. Please start from the beginning." Samuel said as he pushed the record button on the recorder.

Jones sits back in his chair and begin. "We got a call from the Founders Hotel on Broadway that there had been a murder. When we arrived at the crime scene, we quickly realized that it was anything but just a murder. The room was covered in blood and body parts of men, women and even children. It was nothing like I have ever seen before. I met your father that day. He was an awesome detective who paid attention to details and was very thorough. Doctor Hal was the coroner back then. He was not equipped to handle such massive load of bodies yet along process them in the timely manner that was needed. For that, the Governor called in the New York Bureau of Investigation to help us. Normally we locals would have been offended and put off by the NYBI interfering with our cases, but this time we welcomed all the help we could get. Also, there was not all the technology that you spoiled guys have today," Jones said with laughter.

"Things were done manually and slowly back then. The bodies had been ripped apart. There were no clean cuts. The coroner determined that they were alive at the time. Cause of death was dismemberment and massive blood loss. A total of sixty-four men, women and children. No one saw them enter the hotel. No one heard the cries or struggles. There were guests in the rooms on both sides of the crime scene room. It was as if the people appeared in the room and someone hit the mute button while they ripped and tore their bodies apart. The oldest victim was seventy-two, and the youngest victim was eight. It was a sad, sickening feeling in all of our stomachs when we found heads, legs, and arms of children. What kind of sick psycho could do something like that? At first, we thought that the guest had to be lying. Someone heard something, saw something and was scared to say anything. We never got any information that gave us an insight into the how's and why's the massacre occurred. However, there were a lot of strange things happening around us. My partner and I had just helped two local cops catch a young black kid on foot. Boy was he fast. If we did not know a shortcut that would cut him off, we would have never caught him in a straight out chase. Once we caught him and had him in handcuffs, it was like not only his body language and facial expressions changed, but his voice and personality did as well. He had a more sinister look on his face with a taunting grin as well. He said in a deep gruff downright scary ass voice 'So detective, how is your case coming? Did you solve the sixty-four murders yet?' I was taken back a moment. I looked up, and he was looking at me, but his eyes had changed. They were a different dark color, which predominant one I could not tell you. I just knew something was off about them. I ran over to the young man and grabbed him. I asked him what he knew about my case, but when I looked at him again, I could tell he was back to normal. My partner heard and seen the same thing. We decided to leave it out of our report. We didn't want anyone to think we were losing it. That was a stressful case for us all. Lack of sleep, food, and hell even drink except for coffee were taking a toll on us all. If it weren't for coffee, the whole law enforcement team would have been dehydrated."

"Samuel, the memories of all the body parts of men, women and especially children haunts me to this day. The biggest haunting of the past came from when my partner and I investigated a murder of a priest and a nun at a Catholic church that was in the same block as the hotel where the mass murders took place. Someone had stripped them of their clothes except for the priest's shirt and collar and the nun's habit. They both had strange marking brunt all over their bodies. Their rosaries had been shelved into their mouth. Their bodies hung upside down on inverted crosses, and their carotid arteries were cut. They bled to death while hanging there. Samuel, they were alive, tortured and hung in a ritualistic way in a holy church by some sadistic psycho who I was never able to catch. As I said, it haunts me to this day. I hope you can bring closure to your case and find the bastards who did this. I know I'm not that helpful, but if any questions come up that you need to ask me, please call anytime day or night," Jones said finishing his statement.

Samuel waited a few seconds before responding to make sure that Jones did not want to add anything else.

"You have helped me more than you realize," Samuel finally responded. "The missing blood alone is a revelation that we all missed. Thank you so much for coming out here at such short notice." Samuel said while leaning forward and shutting off the tape recorder.

"I will be in town for two more days. I decided to visit some old friends while I am here. If you need anything else or have any more questions, please don't hesitate to call me on my cell phone, day or night," said Jones.

"I will. Thank you. I'll give you a ride back to your hotel," Samuel replied.

"No, I am going to visit some old colleagues in the area. I will take a cab back when I'm finished. Samuel," Jones said in a low voice while stepping closer to Samuel "Be careful. My gut tells me that this time it's gravely dangerous for all involved," he warned Samuel while staring at him intently.

"I will Jones. I will." Samuel said as he extended his hand out for a farewell handshake.

As Jones leaves the room, Samuel could not help but think he is right. This time is different. This time there may be more lives lost than just the ones that were lost in the hotel room. If he is not careful and vigilant, it could be his life Samuel thought to himself as his stomach turns into a knot.

For three days and nights the demon father, Jacob and demon mother, Telsa have been tortured at the command and hands of Mistress. Mistress enjoyed every excruciating moment of it. A normal human body would have perished days before, but these bodies have demons inside of them, which enabled the bodies to endure and remain functional under extreme torturous circumstances due to the quick healing powers of the demons. All that did was prolong the inevitable death in the end.

"Was it worth it?" Mistress asks Jacob in a calm, soft voice.

Jacob did not answer at first. When Mistress does not get a response, she glances over at Jacob. As she stares at him, he cries out in pain. Mistress smiles.

"Now answer me when I ask you something or the next time it will be Telsa in pain," she commanded him.

" No, it was not worth it," Jacob managed to say between clinched bloody teeth.

Both Jacob and Telsa were naked and handcuffed to a large shiny metal circular ring divided into four equal parts by an X in the center. Each of their legs and arms is handcuffed to each corner where the X connects to the metal circle. Metal handcuffs connect their wrists and ankles with no padding. The cuffs are cutting into their wrists and ankles. They are suspended in the air, which increased the pain and cuts due to the force of their body weight on their bondage.

Mistress looks at the blood pooling on the floor under Jacob and Telsa and smiles.

"Every little bit counts," she whispers to herself.

Gabe, her first lieutenant, comes into the room followed by two-second lieutenants, Tonya and Dale. Gabe's long wavy brown hair flows behind him, which falls to his mid-back. If there is such a thing as ambrosia to the eyes, he would be it. He stands six feet five inches tall with an athletic well defined muscular body. He has a smile that is both alluring and causes someone to let his or her guard down. He is the perfect killing machine with no conscious. He is only second to Mistress in his cruelty and demonic behavior. Gabe worships Mistress like no other. His loyalty is unconditional, unquestioning, and fierce. Anyone who questions, challenges or is disloyal to Mistress will be eliminated with great pleasure by Gabe. To him, she is a GODDESS.

Gabe walks over to Mistress and kneels down on one knee before her. He is the only one who is allowed to kneel on one knee before Mistress. All others have to kneel on both knees before her to show their submissiveness and obedience. Mistress is very fond of Gabe. He is her favorite. Gabe loves Mistress very much. He is borderline in love with her. While Mistress cares deeply for Gabe, she is nowhere near in love with him. One would even question if Mistress is capable of loving anyone, but herself. Her feelings for Gabe are one of the closest feelings she has ever experienced when it comes to almost loving another demon. She has only cared for one other demon in her millions of years of existence. Even though she is very fond of Gabe, he is nowhere near her equal in anyone's mind especially hers. For everyone is submissive to Mistress. No exceptions.

Mistress walks over to Gabe and touches his cheek while running her fingers gently down to his chin. She gently lifts his head up, so he can gaze into her eyes. They both smile at each other once their eyes meet. Gabe's mind and demonic soul belong entirely to Mistress. There is no doubt in her mind that she controls and owns every part of his mind, demon soul, and existence. The sight of him is very pleasing to her eyes.

The second lieutenants kneeled on both of their knees, one on each side of Gabe. Mistress did not even acknowledge them. They expected as such. After all, they are here for her pleasure and to serve her desires only. Just being in her presence is enough for them.

Mistress's touch intoxicates Gabe. One might think he is about to pass out by looking at him. Mistress lowers her hand from Gabe's face and turns her attention back to Jacob and Telsa. While looking at them, she starts to talk to only Gabe even though there are over twenty other demons in the large gym size room.

"Gabe do you think I am a just Mistress?" she asked.

Gabe loves hearing her call his name. His eyes rolled back in his heard and slightly closed at the sound of her voice calling his name.

"Yes Mistress, very just," he replied.

"Do you think I am a fair Mistress?" she asked.

"Yes Mistress, very fair," he replied.

"Do I not allow all to live in peace under my protection? Do I not allow each demon to pursue happiness as he or she sees fit as long as they serve me and my needs first and far most?" she asked in a slightly louder voice than before.

"Yes, Mistress you do," Gabe answered.

"Then why would these two ungrateful ass wipes betray me the way they did?" she asked even louder than before.

"Yes it is an act of betrayal!" she yelled out before Gabe could respond.

"Yes, it is an act of betrayal Mistress," Gabe echoed her sentence in his own words.

"An act of betrayal!" she yelled out in anger.

The air grows dense and heavy from her angry powers. Mistress feels herself getting upset. She makes a conscientious effort to stabilize herself and calm back down. Everyone in the room is trembling with fear, even Gabe. If Mistress does not contain her anger, her powers could kill all in the room unintentionally. As Mistress speaks in a calm contained voice, the air became thinner. Everyone in the room except the two prisoners breathes out a sigh of relief.

"Jacob and Telsa. Telsa and Jacob," Mistress sang in a playful chorus.

"What shall I do with you now?" she asked herself talking to no one in general, not even Gabe. Then a smile comes over her face. A sinister kind of smile that has Jacob concerned. She motions for her servants to take them down off the metal circles by pointing to the floor while looking at Jacob and Telsa. Two men went to each of the prisoners and began to remove them from the high metal circles.

"She is dead," one of the demons informed Mistress.

The room is silent and waiting for Mistress to respond. Jacob brakes the silence and begins to sob. This is not what Mistress wants. She wants to torture her some more. She bled out too much. Mistress feels herself getting pissed because she feels as though she has been robbed of her revenge. She has to take a deep breath to make herself calm down. In her process of making herself calm down, Mistress overcompensates and releases her power on Jacob that prevents him from escaping the human body, which should have been okay since another demon is assigned to mentally ensure that Jacob does not leave the human body as well. Before Mistress and everyone realize what has happened, Jacob leaves the human body as fast as he could.

His anger and pain are unbearable. Not only has he lost his daughter, but he has also lost the only one who he had every loved. He lost Telsa. Mistress will pay for this he promises himself. He knew too much for them to let him live. After all, he is a second lieutenant of Mistress as well. She does not know the meaning of betrayal Jacob thought to himself. No, not even a little bit. I will be an excellent tool for the destruction of all that you hold dear and then the destruction of you Mistress as well Jacob thought to himself. He found an old man with an unkempt beard sitting on his front porch. He went inside his body. He leaned over and cried like a two-year-old child.

Michael waits a few minutes before speaking. He wants her to adjust to her surroundings while especially adjusting to the realization that he is real. All of it is real. He needs her to have a semi leveled head before he tries to explain things to her again. After a few minutes passed, Michael speaks in a soft, soothing tone of voice "Auroa, my name is Michael. I am an angel sent to guide and protect you."

"Yes, yes you said that before. Guide and protect me from what?" Auroa managed to ask.

"There is a war that is about to start. A war between demons, humans, and angels. Good and evil. Humans will fight the bulk of the war. Angels can only play a minimal roll in this war, such as training, protecting the key human fighters and guiding them in the decisions that they have to make and carry out." Michael explained.

"Why do you need me? Why do you need humans?" Auroa asked bewildered.

"It is because of free will. Humans have inherited the earth. They are the ones who must choose good over evil. The angels cannot make that choice for them. As long as you choose good, I will be your protector, your guide, and your confidant in the battles to come." Michael explained.

Auroa sits up on the couch and steadies herself as she slides all the way back on the cushions. This is insane she thought to herself. Has she really went off on the deep end and lost her marbles completely? She feels like asking herself if she took her medication, but she does not take medication. Well now would be a good time to start she thought to herself. Michael senses her struggle to make sense of everything. He sits in silence to give her time for all that he had said to sink in. For a moment it looks as though Auroa is going to pass out again, but she holds true and stays awake.

"Michael I think you have the wrong person. I am no leader, and I'm definitely not fighting in any war," she explained trying to steady her voice the best she could without shouting at the top of her lungs.

"No Auroa, I have the right person. You are the one. You are the only one who got an angel to protect you all to yourself. All the people in the park were your lieutenants. They got one angel to forty lieutenants. You, on the other hand, are the head. You are the leader. I am here just for you. My sole job is to protect and guide you from this point on." Michael spoke slowly in a low voice to try to calm Auroa as much as he could.

Auroa sits for a few minutes in silence while not saying a word. Michael gives Auroa a few minutes to stabilize herself. He understands that it is a lot to take in for a human. Even though they are in perilous times, they are not pressed for time. He has time for her to acclimate herself to all that has transpired. While he sits across the room at the small dining room table, he takes advantage of the moment to really look at her. Auroa's fair skin with rosy cheeks and short brown semi-curly wavy hair give her an innocent alluring look. Her voluptuous body is not frail. She has beautiful, alluring curves to go with her alluring face that genuinely disarms a man in her presence. She is just plain beautiful to look at. Michael studies Auroa's reaction, her facial features, body language and small gestures she makes with her hands to her face and lap as she tries to let her brain comprehend the events of the day. Even though it appears that she is genuinely having a hard time coming to grips with the reality of the day, she is handling it a lot better than Michael thought she would. This is not Michael's first time acting as a sole ambassador to the leader of a war against evil. Michael, an Archangel, has been around since the dawn of time. He has counseled thousands of leaders in the past. Only five have yielded to the dark side and chose the path of evil instead of good. As long as Auroa chooses good over evil, light over darkness, he will be by her side through it all. Many will be lost in this war, some to death and some to evil. However, he will be her steadfast rock to lean on and guide her through it all. There will come a time when Auroa will be tempted. A time will come when she has to make a choice. He prays that her character and soul are strong enough to withstand the temptations to come. For if she chooses evil, he will be the one chosen to kill her. That would be a sad day for Michael indeed.

Ten days before the ritual by Mistress and Lucifer that would start the war between humans and demons, every demon was ordered to kill one person per night around the world each night before the ritual. The first kill of the night is the most important one. The souls of the first kills go to hell for one day, which is a lifetime, to be tortured into accepting to fight for Lucifer's army. They have to say yes. If they do not accept the invitation to fight for Lucifer at the end of the day, they will be made whole again and brought back to life. Their memory of what had happened when they were killed and afterward would be gone. The first kill of the night is a good person. They are people who are heaven bound. Lucifer and Mistress have a sadistic sense of humor. Also, for every soul that is converted to fight for Lucifer, the demon side gets to bring back to life one fallen demon who had died in battle. It does not apply to the demons who are second Lieutenants or higher. It refers to low ranking demons only.

Tonight a demon has set his eyes on Linda for the first kill of the night. Linda is a good-hearted woman who loves God very much. She goes to church, helps her fellow man and woman any way she can and always sees the good in everyone regardless of their past or current status. She is a light for a lot of people in the dark places they call their lives.

Tonight is uncannily warm for this time of year. There is no breeze tonight. No small bug sounds filling the air. Just the sounds of Linda and her friend talking to each other as they leave the little mom and pop cafe they ate dinner at together while laughing and enjoying each other's company. Linda had arrived in the area almost an hour before her friend did, so she had parked far away from near the small shops that line the new four-lane highway. They did not decide where to eat until her friend had arrived.

They both embrace in the parking lot of the cafe. After turning down a ride to her car by her friend, Linda starts to walk along the semi-deserted sidewalk casually. The neighborhood she is in is relatively safe with no crimes reported in ages. Therefore, Linda feels perfectly safe as she relaxes and walks unwittingly of the danger that is not only watching her but intends to take her life violently very soon. The demon watches her intently in its invisible form as Linda passes it along the sidewalk. Mistress will be very pleased it thought to itself. It does not attack her right away. It wants to take its time and relish in the moment. It does not need to chase her or worry about her getting too far away. After all, she cannot outrun him, and he has caught her scent. Only a miracle could save her now, yes only a miracle. What the demon does not know is that he is being watched too. A miracle is watching him while waiting for Linda to walk a distance away from him. It is the Archangel Raphael. Linda has a guardian angel tonight, a very powerful guardian angel.

Just before the demon is about to strike Linda down, Raphael reveals his presence to the demon.

"She is not for you demon," Raphael said in a voice that sounded like music and not audible to Linda.

"Who do you think..." the demon started to reply but stopped midsentence when he realized who he was talking to.

Raphael knows he cannot let the demon live. It has the scent of Linda, and it will never stop hunting her until she is dead, even if she is not the first kill of the night.

"You have no right to deny us our prize." the demon said in a shaky voice while backing away from Raphael to put some distance between the two of them.

"Deny I will and kill you I must," Raphael replied while closing the gap between them.

The demon tried to turn and run away.

"Stay," ordered Raphael as he walks up close to the demon who is now unable to move or flee.

"She is not for you Mistress. She belongs to God. Do not attempt to kill her again." Raphael ordered while giving an unspoken warning at the same time. Mistress heard the words and is instantly angered as well as scared of the Archangel. She will leave Linda alone for now. Mistress knows she cannot save her servant even though it cries out her name for help just before the Archangel sets his inner being on fire and destroys him.

Linda continues to walk down the now deserted sidewalk oblivious to what just transpired as well as to her escape of death and torture at the hands of pure evil. Raphael takes the body which the demon occupied with him so he can discard it. This safe, quiet neighborhood will remain just that, quiet and safe, at least for tonight.

It is always nice to be home Jordan thought as she walks through the front door of her home. Jordan, a CIA undercover operative, travels a lot throughout the year. She is away often. Jordan hates to be away from her husband and two young boys, Matthew who is three and Alex who is two. Her family does not know that she works for the CIA. Also, they do not know that she is now a first lieutenant on the good side for the fight for all humanity against evil. So many secrets, but somehow she keeps it all together yet separate. Once it was two separate lives that she lived, but now its three separate lives of family, CIA and now a first lieutenant. What a web we weave when we web to deceive she thought as she places her traveling bags on the floor in the foyer. The family's best friend, Paul, was looking after her kids when she came home, which was not abnormal. He helps out her and her husband a lot. The boys call and think of him as an uncle. He is a good cook as well. He just finished making a dinner of Filet mignon, fried shrimps, bake potato and a Caesar salad. Save the steak; it is one of Jordan's favorite meals. Paul set the table and beckons her to join him. The boys have already eaten earlier. Jordan walks over and sits down at one of the end chairs.

"Where is Jack?" she asked Paul.

"He is wrapping up some things at work. He should be home in a couple of hours," he answered Jordan as he brings the nicely arranged plate of food over to her and sits it in front of her.

Jordan picks up one of the shrimps and dips it in the cocktail sauce. She savors the taste of it in her mouth.

"Where are Matthew and Alex?" she asked. "Are they sleeping?"

"No" replied Paul. "they are in the other room playing. You should eat first. Once they see you, you will not be able to eat. They won't let you." he advised her.

Jordan knows he is right. She cuts the red parts away for the tender steak. She does not like it rare. The cooked portion of the steak is so tender, tasty and juicy. One cannot go wrong with fried shrimp, but Paul took the spices to another level. They were perfect. Jordan finished the meal and glass of wine set before her while enjoying Paul's company laced with lots of laughter. Paul was like the brother she never had. Her husband, Tom and her met Paul in college. He was the best man at their wedding and is the godfather of their children. They love him very much. Paul loves them as well. He treats their children as if they are his own. If something ever happens to them, they will be his. In their will, they gave custody of the boys to him. After all, he is the godfather. After dinner Jordan goes into the other room to watch her youngest son, Alex play. He was having the time of his life in the swing that hangs in the middle of the room. The swing is just low enough for Alex's feet to touch the floor and push off in any direction he wants to. Her other son, Matthew runs into the room to greet her. What a big Cheetos smile on his face she thought to herself as he runs full speed across the room towards her. He jumps into her arms. She catches him in midair, and they both fall back onto the couch laughing.

"I've missed you!" she yelled out.

"I've missed you too!" he yelled in return.

They both hug and kiss each other while laughing with great happiness in each other arms. Alex is watching from the swing with a great big smile on his face.

"Matthew watch this!" he yelled out as he pushes as hard as he can with his legs that sent him far up into the air.

Jordan and Matthew cheer Alex on from the couch. Today is a good day thought Jordan. These are the days I live for she thought to herself. A good day for sure. She feels such peace today. At that moment Paul enters the room with five other men and Jordan's husband badly beaten. Her husband, Jack, is being held up in a standing position by two of the men. Something is wrong. She instinctively picks up Matthew and runs to Alex.

She kneels down to Matthew and says "I need you to stand here and don't move. I need you to protect your brother. Can you do that for me no matter what happens?" she asked him.

"Yes," Matthew said through tears.

Matthew knows something is very wrong. His father is hurt. He can see the fear in the eyes of his most favorite person in the world, his mother. Jordan stands up and runs to her husband. His face is bloody. His left hand had three fingers missing. He could barely walk.

"What happened?" she screamed out asking her husband.

Jack replies "Paul."

She looks confused.

"What?" she asked in disbelief and an almost in a state of shock.

"Paul happened," he whispered through bloody lips.

Instantly her fear turns into anger. She stands and faces Paul.

"You did this?" she asked between clenched teeth.

Paul had a cocky smile on his face.

"As a matter of fact I did, well I had it done to him while I watched," he answered her.

"Why?' she asked getting more and more angrier by the second.

"Because I thought he was someone else. However, he is not the one, you are." Paul answered her. "You are the first lieutenant of the angels, not your husband."

Jordan is shocked that Paul knows this. She had kept things so secretive. She was careful during her meetings with the angels and others except for the day in the park when the angels first appeared.

"What are you talking about?" she tried to sound as if she didn't know what he was talking about.

"Don't play with me Jordan or the next ones to be tortured will be your children," he warned her.

Jordan instantly goes into the defense mode. Her heart beats faster. Her breathing becomes deeper while her muscles begin to get ready for fight or flight mode. She glances back over her shoulder to make sure that her sons were safe as they can be under these circumstances. She wants to make sure that Matthew is still standing by his brother, which he is. All is how it was supposed to be.

"Why would you do this Paul?" You are like a brother to us." her voice got lower with each word until she ended the sentence with a whisper.

The heartbreak is evident in her voice and facial expression. Her heart breaks more and more with each question that left her lips.

"You think I am Paul. No Jordan I am not Paul. I killed Paul three weeks ago and took over his body. Yes, I have been watching and spending time with your family for three weeks." he answered Jordan as if she had asked him the question with her mind. Can he read thoughts Jordan wondered. No, she concluded because if he could, he would have known she is the first lieutenant and not Jack. The two men let Jack fall to the floor. They start to walk toward Jordan.

"Are you all demons?" she asked.

"Yes," replied Paul as he is walking towards her as well. "My name is Azasar. I'm your counterpart. I am a first lieutenant of Mistress. You joined the wrong side Jordan."

Jordan reaches behind her back under her jacket and pulls out two sharp eight-inch knives out of the holsters. They are knives that the angels gave her. They can kill demons and other supernatural creatures, except for angels. She turns the knives backward in her hands. With one more glance over her shoulders to check on her boys, she goes into a defensive fighting stance.

"A fight you want, a fight you will have," she informed them as the first demon leaps through the air. She meets the demon in mid-air cutting his throat and then resuming her fighting stance.

"Why are you fighting Jordan? You can't win. That was luck." Azasar taunted her.

The best weapon that Jordan has is her best-kept secret training. Azasar does not know her as much as he thinks he knows her. Jordan blocks the left punch of one demon while backward karate kicking another. Azasar looks very surprised at her skills. How is she doing this he thought to himself.

"Get her!" he commanded the remaining two demons.

They both rush Jordan. She sidesteps one while slicing his midsection open. Jordan goes down to one knee and trusts the knife deep into the side of the other demon. With all her strength and might she pulls the blade around to the other side of the midsection. It was not too hard. The knives are very sharp. Both demons fell to the floor. Jordan finishes off the demon with the sliced midsection by a quick stab in the side of the throat and pulls the blade forward resulting in cutting his throat.

"Paul, Paul, Paul," she said to him shaking her head while standing on her feet.

"My name is Azasar! Say it right!" he yelled out to her.

As she starts to walk towards him, Azasar leaves the body and flies out the opened window of the living room. Paul's body falls lifeless to the floor.

"Coward," Jordan whispered.

She quickly holsters her knives. She runs over to her children to make sure they are okay. They are crying, but okay. Frighten, but okay. Jordan runs over to Jack.

"Baby I'm so sorry. I'm so sorry. We have to go to the hospital. I can't have them come here. They will see the bodies." Jordan helps Jack to his feet. He moans out in agony.

"I'm sorry, I'm sorry." she kept saying to Jack. "Stay here while I put Daddy in the car. I'll be right back." She helps Jack out to the car. After buckling him in the front seat, she runs back inside the house to get the boys. Good soldiers. They both followed her orders and didn't move Jordan thought to herself.

"Good job, I am so proud of you both." she praised them.

What will this do to them she thought. Please God protect their innocence. Please protect our children she prays silently to herself while gathering up the diaper bag.

Mistress is not pleased. She is not pleased at all. Not only has she been robbed of her pleasure of inflicting unimaginable pain on Jacob, but he was a valuable asset to her defense and her team of fighters. The knowledge that he has could be crippling, to say the least, if it gets into the wrong hands. He has to be found and eliminated at all cost.

"Gabe!" she called out.

Within a minute Gabe is present and kneeling before her.

"What the hell just happened, Gabe? Why did your demons let him escape? Did I not tell you to order them to have a mental inhibitor on them to prevent them from escaping the bodies at all times? Did you not inform your demons of this?" Mistress yelled out the questions in anger.

The objects in the room start to shake. At the end of her questioning, the very building begins to shake as well. Dust fills the air from a crack in the ceiling. Mistress takes a deep breath to calm herself before she brings her beloved building down around them. Gabe knows not to speak right away with excuses. They will only infuriate her more. He kneels in silence while Mistress mentally calms herself. Once she feels she has calmed down enough, she takes a deep breath and deliberately focus and speaks in a calm voice.

"Gabe, what happened? Who did you assign to concentrate on keeping him contained in the body?" Mistress seems remarkably composed, yet underneath she is mad as hell. She waits for Gabe to respond, which seems like a lifetime to her.

"I'm not sure what happen Mistress." he started to reply.

She interrupts him and snaps "You better get sure and know very very soon!"

Even though Gabe is her favorite, He knows to choose his words very carefully.

"Yes Mistress, I will figure it out and inform you in a timely manner," he replied humbly.

"Don't make me ask my second question again," she warned him.

"Fredrick was in charge of keeping Jacob in his body. Another demon was in charge of keeping Telsa in her body, which he did." Gabe informed her.

"Bring Fredrick to me. Now!" she said in a low voice between clenched teeth.

"Do I have permission to leave your presence Mistress?" Gabe asked as he looks up at his Mistress's face.

"You may go," she answered him quietly.

Gabe stands up and walks out of the room as fast as he could. Mistress does not like to be kept waiting. His only desire is to please her. When she is not pleased, he feels like he has failed. Someone has hell to pay for making Mistress upset as well as causing him to fail her. They will pay with their life.

He walks through the long stony airy corridor. He comes to an oversized red metal door with the engravings of ancient demonic symbols on it. He stops for a moment to contain his anger. He wants to rip Fredrick a new asshole, but that would not please Mistress. He takes a deep calming breath before opening the door. The red metal door opens up to the middle section of the six section building. The building is a twenty story old welled preserved stone castle nestled inside a mountain in Colorado. Over time it has been overtaken by the natural environment of the mountain that hides it from the rest of the world. Mistress had used her powers to restore the interior and physical structure of the building fully. Solid and majestic, it is now the home to thousands of demons. It is filled with demon men, women and children. The castle has hundreds of corridors, rooms and hidden passageways.

Gabe instantly tunes in on Fredrick but steadies himself to keep himself contained from not running over to rip his head off his shoulders at first sight of him. There are about sixty demons in the football field size room scattered about here and there. Gabe walks slowly and deliberately over to where Frederick is standing. Frederick knows what Gabe is probably there for. He knows that they figured it out that he broke his concentration while watching Jacob. What they didn't know was that Jacob was his best friend. What Jacob didn't know was that he was lovers with Telsa. When Frederick saw that Telsa had died, he lost his concentration. He was in love with her. She loved Jacob more. She would never leave Jacob. It was hard on them both to keep it a secret and even harder keeping it from Mistress. Her secret died with her as his secret will die with him.

"What happen Fredrick?" Gabe asked in the calmest voice he could muster under the current circumstances.

"I lost my concentration," Frederick replied.

He knew what Gabe was asking about.

"Apparently." Gabe agreed between clenched teeth. "Why did you lose concentration that ended up letting Jacob escape as a result?" he asked Frederick.

"I don't know Gabe. It just happened. I looked away for a moment, and he must have felt my gaze leave him. He seized the moment to leave his host." Frederick tried to explain.

Frederick knows that his faith was already sealed. He knows Mistress will kill him personally and that it would be catastrophic in the magnitude of torture that will end in his death. However, Frederick does not want that to happen. He has one more card to play. One more grand finale. A demon has the power within itself to kill itself by sheer thought, as long as it is not being suppressed within the host by another demon who is more powerful than it is. It is very painful and takes a few minutes. Frederick had started the process time he saw Gabe walk into the room. It is nothing short of a demon miracle that he can do so while continuing to answer Gabe's questions calmly.

"Mistress is not pleased," Gabe informed him. "You let her prisoner, her second lieutenant who has a wealth of knowledge escape. If he gets into the wrong hands, it could undermine all that we have been trying to accomplish, if not debacle it completely." Gabe said as he started to close the gap between them.

"I am sorry for my shortcomings Gabe. I am, I am sorry I failed Mistress. I failed you." he apologized as humbly as he could.

Gabe is not here for his apologies. He does not want his apologies. He wants his life. He wants him to suffer for displeasing Mistress as well as himself. Gabe is about three feet from Fredrick, and then he realizes what is going on. Gabe is too late as he takes another step to close the gap between the two of them, Frederick's knees buckle, and he falls to the floor dead with his eyes still open.

"Dammit!" Gabe yelled. "Mistress is going to be furious," he said out loud while dreading being the one to tell her.

Samuel is tired. He has not slept in thirty-six hours. His mind is getting slower, and his body is beginning to shut down. Thomas looks over the desk and thinks to himself that the dead can walk, talk and breathe.

"Go lay down man. I'll let you know if something comes up. You're no good to me or anyone else if you can't think and function properly." he said to Samuel.

He has been saying similar suggestions to Samuel for the past three hours off and on. This time Samuel decides it would be best if he listens.

"Okay." he finally said after a long pause. "You have my number if you want to get in touch with me. "

Samuel gets up and goes over to the fax machine to make sure no new information has come in for him first. A sigh of disappointment escapes from him when he realizes nothing is there. He grabs his coat and reminds Thomas to call him if there is a new development as he walks out the door.

"Yea I'm all over that. Get some rest Mr. Zombie." Thomas mumbled to himself out of earshot of Samuel.

As Samuel leaves the building, he has an urge to go see Father Hanningan. He does not know why. He just knows he would not be able to rest until he did so. The parking garage is deserted this time of morning. 2:00 am does come fast when you're busy he thought to himself as he walks through the door to the stairwell that leads down the to the third level. As he exits the staircase, he feels someone watching him. He turns out of instinct, and there was a man behind him. The man is over six feet tall with light brown hair and the most unusual dark green eyes Samuel has ever seen. He is wearing a black knee length leather coat that almost looked like it was made just for his body frame. He is wearing a red shirt and black pants that also look like they were tailored made. The man is about three feet behind Samuel. How could he had not heard or seen him coming down the stairwell Samuel thought to himself.

"Good morning," Samuel said to the tanned face man with the goatee.

"Good morning." the man replied in a voice that had an accent of another language besides English to it.

Samuel could not place the accent. Instinctively Samuel walks at an angle that would eliminate the man being directly behind him so close. However, the man matches his steps. When Samuel changes his angle of approach again, the man changes his as well. Samuel increases his walking pace, and the man does the same. Samuel turns around and is surprised that no one is there.

"What the hell," he said out loud in disbelief. Am I that tired he thought to himself.

As he turns around the man is right in front of him less than a half a foot away. He is so close that Samuel could not take one step forward. Samuel jumps from being startled. Before he could say anything, the man just disappears right before his eyes. What is going on Samuel asks himself silently in his head. I am so tired that I am hallucinating now he thought. Samuel is now borderline running to his car. As he pulls out of the parking garage, all he could think about is that I've got to see Father Hannigan.

The hospital room is quiet except for the constant heartbeat sound of the heart monitor. They saved Jack's life. Jordan is so grateful. Yes so grateful indeed. She has not left her husband's side with her children. The CIA and the hospital gave him a private suite that is reserved for very important people with beds and supplies for her and the boys, which enables her to stay with Jack around the clock. The CIA has given her 24 hours around the clock protection that is posted outside the door of the hospital suite. She can breathe, sleep and relax as a result of the 24 hours protection detail. Jack was touch and go there for a minute. The hospital staff worked to resuscitate him twice. Each time a little of Jordan died with him. She could not imagine life without her rock, her soul mate. She needs him so much more than he needs her and yet he treats her like she is the center of his universe. In all actuality, he is clearly the center of hers.

With everything going on, Jordan does not have time to meet secretly with the other first lieutenants or their assigned angel. She has other things at the forefront of her mind. Her life and healthy state of mind almost came to an abrupt end. She thanked God for his grace and healing hand in saving Jack. There is a knock at the door. One of the security detail agents informs Jordan that she has a visitor. It is a detective.

"Okay let him in," Jordan replied.

To her surprise, it was the Archangel Raphael, the angel assigned to her group of forty Lieutenants who walks into the room. He is dressed in all white that contrast against his mocha chocolate colored skin. His features are well defined with eyes that seem to look into your soul, if not entirely through you. The sight of him caught Jordan off guard.

"Hello, Jordan." Raphael greeted her.

Jordan has to clear her throat first. "Ra Raphael, I didn't expect to see you here," she said clearly surprised.

"I know. Since you couldn't come to me, I decided to come to you," Raphael said.

"I could not leave his side." Jordan started to explain.

"I know," Raphael said in an understanding manner.

Raphael walks over to the bed where Jack is lying hooked up to the cardiac monitors and IV bag. He stops at the foot of the bed. Matthew and Alex stare at Raphael in silence and awe with both of their mouths open. Jordan is so surprised that the two of them are so quiet with total attention on Raphael. Raphael glances down at the two boys and smiles a smile that would not only stop traffic but touch a person's soul as well. Jordan watches as Raphael looks at Jack. What she does not know is that Raphael is communicating with Jack in his mind.

"Jack, my name is Raphael. I am an Archangel. I know you have been through a great ordeal. I am here to heal you, but before I do, I want to tell you some things that I need you to know. There is a battle going on. Good versus evil. Your wife is one of the ones enlisted to lead in the fight against evil. She will play a vital part in the long run in this fight. We need her to be focused and giving one hundred percent of her attention and skills to help us win the battles to come. I won't lie to you. There will be casualties on both sides, whether to death or evil. We, the angels, as well as the other leaders of the good side, want to minimize these casualties. I can see that you love Jordan very much and she loves you as well. Therefore, I am going to heal you back to your state of being before you were tortured. In return, I need you to be there for Jordan. I need you to be her rock more than ever. Be there for the children. Take care of things, so Jordan doesn't have to worry. Free up her mind so she can concentrate on the tasks at hand. I will erase everyone's memory of the events except you and Jordan. Your children will not remember as well. I will restore the life of your best friend, Paul because he will be needed by you and Jordan to help take care of things. We can't have her mind on the loss of Paul when other grave matters need her attention to detail. Do you understand and agree to the terms I have set to heal you?" asked Raphael in Jack's head.

"Yes, I do, and I agree to do everything in my power to be there and support Jordan to enable her to be a success. Thank you. Thank you so very much. Thank you, Jesus. Thank you." Jack replied silently.

Jordan does not know what was going on. She just sits there watching Raphael stand perfectly still at the foot of her husband's bed looking silently down at him for what seemed like forever. For some reason, she does not have the desire to interrupt him. Raphael turns to Jordan and tells her the same things that he said to Jack in his mind. Jordan could not thank Raphael enough. She said it over and over through tears, while intermittingly thanking God as well. Raphael just smiled and said "The Lord's grace shines on you and your family Jordan. You are truly one of his chosen ones."

With that, he touched the leg of Jack. Instantly the family is back at their home. Jack is healed and whole again. After a moment of surprise, Jack and Jordan embrace each other crying. They hold each other tightly and fall to the couch crying. They are both truly grateful for the blessings and second chance they have been given.

Gabe is furious that he does not have a chance to torture Fredrick for his shortcomings for not only disappointing Mistress, but for disappointing him as well. However, he has more pressing matters at hand. Gabe has to figure out how to tell Mistress that Fredrick killed himself. He has to disappoint her again. Make her mad and lethal. He does not like disappointing her. He definitely does not like making her angry or lethal. He knows from experience that Mistress will kill the one that brings her bad news of this magnitude. Therefore, he decides it will not be him. He cannot keep her waiting. Gabe walks across the room to a ten-foot-high metal and mahogany door. He pushes it open and sees Laiya, a low ranking oblivious demon. Just what he needs he thought to himself. She needs to be oblivious to what is going to happen to her if she brings Mistress terrible news. It really helps that she has not had much interaction with Mistress or seen what she is capable of when she is mad.

"Hello, Laiya. What are you working on?" he asked her before she could reply with a greeting back.

"Nothing at the moment," she replied.

Laiya has always been a puppet demon who does not show initiative or has any drive to excel in the ranks. She would not be a loss at all Gabe thought to himself.

"I have a task for you to do and it must be completed immediately," he informed her.

"Okay," she replied

"I need you to go tell Mistress that Frederick has killed himself," he informed her.

"What?" she asked surprised. "Why would Frederick?" she started to ask, but Gabe interrupts her.

"The why and what is not important," he informed her. "Go and do as you are told and inform Mistress at once," he said in a commanding voice sending her to her death for sure.

"Yes Sir at once," she replied and hurried through the mahogany and metal door.

He is going to wait until he sees the lights go dim throughout the building. For that is when he would know that Mistress has used great powers to accomplish an enormous task such as killing a demon while enraged. Sure enough in a matter of minutes, the lights do the tell-tell sign of Mistress being Mistress. Shortly after another demon steps into the room and says to Gabe "Mistress would like to see you." Gabe takes a deep breath and walks very slowly to see Mistress. He wants to give her time to calm down. The more time he gives her, the calmer she would be. As he makes it to Mistress's chamber, he takes a moment to take a deep breath before entering the room.

"Yes Mistress," he said in a very soft submissive voice.

"It was very wise of you to send me that message by someone else. It seems you have grown in your decision-making skills and know me well in some areas," she praised Gabe's judgment, which surprised Gabe. He expected her to be furious. However, her mood is quite the opposite. Then he realized that Mistress is satisfied with the pain and suffering she had caused on Laiya. She is actually sexually turned on by it. Mistress walks over to where Gabe is kneeling on one knee. She touches his face gently with her fingers. Gabe lets out a moan of pleasure as he leans into her touch. She gently caresses his cheeks and then firmly grabs his chin with one hand while she pulls his head back hard by the hair with the other hand. Gabe submits completely while becoming sexually aroused as well. Mistress leans down and kisses Gabe passionately on the lips. Both let out a moan of pleasure as she ravishes his mouth with her tongue and lips. She lifts Gabe to his feet by his hair while continuing to kiss and taste him. She leads him over to her bed and forcefully pushes him down in the sitting position at the foot of the bed. Mistress takes her diamond stud collar and leash off its hook from the bedpost and places it around Gabe's neck. Gabe feels himself precum a little as a result. Mistress stands up and leads Gabe around the bed by the collar. These are the moments he lives for, to serve and please Mistress in every way. Gabe stands by the bed waiting to do whatever his Mistress pleases. Starting with his neck, Mistress begins to kiss and taste his skin while undressing him at the same time. As she unbuttons his shirt exposing his nipples, she licks and nibbles on each nipple. She circles the nipple with her tongue before engulfing it in her mouth and sucking very hard. Gabe lets out a cry of pleasure as Mistress bites down on his nipple hard almost breaking the skin. He wants to touch Mistress so bad his body aches. However, he knows he has to wait until she gives him permission to do so. Mistress lets his shirt fall to the floor. She reaches down and unbuckles his pants. In one swift movement, she pulls down his pants to his ankles, which takes her to her knees as well. Gabe is fully aroused. He is absolutely gorgeous Mistress thought to herself. She loves the fact that he is well endowed. He is nine inches of an endowment to be exact and very thick from shaft to the tip of his cock. Mistress lets out a moan of pleasure at the sight of him. Knowing that she is pleased excites Gabe even more. He lets a small amount of precum escape the tip of his cock. At first, Mistress licks the tip tasting his precum on her tongue while enjoying the feeling of it on her lips. She circles the head of his cock with her tongue before engulfing him deep within her mouth and throat while occasionally sucking and circling the head of his cock with her tongue off and on. Gabe's body and mind submit completely to the pleasure of Mistress sucking, tasting and caressing his cock with her hot wet mouth. Mistress cups his balls with one hand at first while going up and down on his cock with her mouth in a nice and slow steady rhythm. With the other hand, Mistress grabs the leash and pulls Gabe down to the bed without taking her mouth off of him. Gabe falls backward to the bed. Mistress continues to taste, suck and caress his cock with her mouth and tongue while pulling him straight on the bed by the leash until his whole body is in bed. While he lays on his back, she inserts one finger into his rectum and starts to massage his prostate while increasing her speed of motion on his cock going in and out of her wet mouth. Gabe's body begins to shake with the pleasure. He explodes deep in her throat. He lets out a loud demonic cry of pleasure while Mistress continues to suck and swallow almost every drop of his cum that escapes the tip of his cock. She holds a small portion of cum in her mouth as she comes up to his lips and snowballs it into his mouth while kissing him passionately.

She tears her lips from his mouth and whispers an order in his ear. "You may touch me now. Pleasure me. I want you to eat me until I tell you to stop. I want to cum in your face and mouth. I want to saturate you with all my juices."

That was the moment Gabe was waiting for. He could hardly contain himself. Mistress loves for him to take control and aggressively take her and pleasure her. She does not want to be handled gently. He can let all of his passion and desire out while pleasing her and taking her as a man should. He becomes aroused again instantly. He rolls Mistress over onto her back while kissing her passionately. He continues to kiss down her neck and stopping at her breast. Mistress loves her breast to be sucked and bitten hard, almost to the point of breaking the skin. She runs her fingers through his hair while moaning and squirming under him with great pleasure. Gabe continues downwards to her stomach while continuing to lick, suck and taste her smooth velvet chocolate skin. He positions himself between her voluptuous thighs enjoying the smell and look of her short trimmed hair on top with completely shaved pussy lips. He could see she is very wet. Mistress always tastes sweet. He loves everything about going down on her. He buries his face between her legs forcing his tongue deep inside her while tasting and feeling her sweet hot sex. Both let out a loud moan of pleasure. As he touches his mouth and tongue on Mistress pussy, she arches her back and lifts off the bed. Gabe knows he is doing it right. He continues to caress her cilt in a circular motion with his tongue while thrusting his tongue deep inside of her off and on. Occasionally he sucks her clit which sends Mistress's body into an uncontrolled state of quivers. She runs her fingers through his hair while pushing his head between her legs until she cannot take any more. She explodes in his mouth, on his tongue, lips, and in his face. He continues to try to lick her while Mistress's body convulses under him. She cannot take any more. She pushes his head away from her sensitive swollen clit. Gabe comes up and begins kissing her passionately as he thrusts his hot throbbing nine inches of cock deep inside her silky wet hot black pussy. He pushes deeper and deeper inside her with every stroke.

He whispers "I am yours and you are mine."

Mistress replies "Yessssssss."

"I have to go to the bathroom," Auroa told Michael.

He looks at her with suspicion. He could read that he has not sold her on the fact that she is the leader in a great war between good and evil, as well as he is her protector, advisor, and confidant throughout it all.

"Unless you want me to go right here," Auroa said in a smart mouth tone.

"No that would not be necessary," replied Michael. "Of course you can go to the bathroom. You are not my prisoner Auroa."

However, that is not how Auroa feels. She feels like she is being held captive in a world wind of a bad dream come true. She stands up and walks slowly in an unsteady gait to the bathroom. She closes the door behind her. Michael continues to sit in the chair at the little table. He thinks about all the preparation and training that need to be done before the fighters, and its lieutenants will be ready for battles. Michael does notice that Auroa took her purse into the bathroom, but he does not think it is unusual for a woman to do so. What he does not know is that Auroa has escaped out the bathroom window. While he sat there thinking about the tasks at hand, Auroa makes her way down the winding walkway to the apartment building parking lot where her car is parked. She fumbles at her keys trying to find the right one. Today has really rattled my nerves she thought to herself as she drives out of the parking lot. She does not want to draw attention to herself, so she obeys all the traffic laws while driving under the speed limit. Her first priority is to get cash. She pulls into her bank's parking lot. She feels very nervous about going inside the bank. She withdraws the maximum amount allowed using a teller machine from her savings account. She should be okay for a couple of days before she would need more she thought to herself. Auroa heads out of town. The evening sky is a beautiful orange and gray color denoting that the sun is going down over the horizon. The night will soon seize the land. It is beautiful and peaceful she thought of the sunset. How could everything else around her be in such turmoil and chaos? She drives the winding road that leads out of town. All of a sudden there is a car that appears behind her from nowhere. She becomes very nervous. She did not notice the headlights there before. It just seemed like they appeared out of thin air. Her body goes into flight mode immediately. Michael, who is still sitting at the table in Auroa's apartment senses Auroa's fear. He jumps to his feet and runs over to the bathroom door. He instantly realizes that she is not in there. He has allowed his mind to be consumed by the thoughts of what is to come that he did not pay attention to Auroa's deception.

He closes his eyes and disappears. He appears in the passenger seat in the car next to Auroa scaring her. She loses control of the car for a brief moment. Michael grabs the wheel and straightens up the car, so it is now driving on the right side of the road.

"Auroa, you are in danger. There are demons in the car behind you. Pull over." he commands her.

"Pull over, are you crazy?" she yelled.

"Auroa, they are no match for me. I am an Archangel. To be in my presence means death to them." he informed her.

She was not listening.

"Pull over!" he commanded in a loud voice that shook the car.

It snaps her back into reality. She slows the vehicle and comes to a stop at the side of the road. The car behind them does the same.

"Stay here. Do not get out of the car for any reason." Michael ordered her.

"Don't worry, I won't," she replied in a shaky voice.

Michael gets out of the vehicle and disappears from Auroa's sight. He walks towards the car that is parked behind them.

"Stay," he commanded, which prohibited the demons from leaving their human host bodies. Realizing who and what he is, the demons try to leave the bodies of the humans. Once they realize that they cannot do so, they try to drive off. The car would not start again. Michael has covered his basis for ensuring that they would not escape. The head lights of the vehicle remain on. The five demons stay in the car. They are scared to get out in the presence of the Archangel. It is not necessary for them to do so. Michael walks over to stand in front of the vehicle headlights. He wants them to see his face as they take their last breath in their human bodies.

"My name is Michael. I know you know who I am. I want my image to be the last thing you see before your human body takes its last breath. I know you have a direct link to your Mistress. Mistress, I am now talking directly to you. Soon this will be your fate." Michael informed her.

Without any effort at all from Michael, the five demons' bodies turn into a bright light inside. Their eyes, mouth, nose, and ears light up. They all scream out in agony and then there is silence. All five are killed at the same time in a matter of seconds.

Michael turns from the bright headlights of the car and walks to the driver side of Auroa's car.

"I'll drive," he informed her.

Auroa slides over to the passenger's seat of the car. Once in the car, Michael addresses Auroa in a calm voice.

"Auroa, you are the leader of this resistance against evil. You have a greater responsibility than you can fathom. True leaders are not ones who waddle in self-pity or only think of themselves.

They look at a problem or situation and figure out how to fix it. They put the whole of the team before the individual. If you don't get it together very soon, this war will be lost before it even starts."

"I'm sorry," Auroa said through tears. "I just thought I needed to get away," she informed him.

"You almost got yourself killed tonight. You cannot be that reckless in the future and expect others to follow you without question, without reservations." Michael scolded Auroa.

"What do I need to do to be a success?" she asked him in a stern convicted voice.

"Asked like a true leader." he praised her as he starts the car and drives into the night back towards the city.

Gregory did not like getting up early in the morning. He always stayed up late playing his video games. Earlier this morning he was awakened by his mother's voice reminding him that he had an appointment to go to this morning. She means well, but he always forgets that in moments when she is waking him up out of a deep peaceful sleep. Even though she warned him last night not to stay up too late, he still gave her attitude when she holds true to her word of 'I am going to wake you up early in the morning, so you better get some rest.' He slept most of the way to and from his appointment earlier that day. He is glad that the ordeal was over, but there is no time for him to play a game today. He promised his friends that he would meet them for a movie and as always, he is running late.

Gregory is a tall thin yet athletic biracial young man. Even though he is mixed with black and white, he always considered himself a black man. Mainly because his mother is black and she has always been his most favorite person in the world. A lot of his great qualities come from his mother. Honesty, loyalty, trustworthy, understanding, leadership, and compassion. He is truly his mother's son, especially in how he treats people and take into account their feelings as well as keeping it real and down to Earth. He is a brilliant young man with great insight as well. He will go far in life not just because his mother always tells him that he will, but because Gregory feels he will as well.

As he walks on the sidewalk at a fast pace to the end of the corner to cross the street to the movie theater, his mind is filled with thoughts of how will he win that armor for his character in his video game. Gregory always felt as though he was born in the wrong time period. He believes he belongs to the medieval or the early Middle Ages of long ago where they fought with swords and body armor. He longs for times of honor, courage, loyalty, and living by a code of the warriors of old. He carries himself with honor as well as that of a natural leader. He is respected and is wise beyond his years. Even his mother notices such qualities in him.

Before Gregory gets to the corner of the sidewalk a man in white appears in front of him. He almost walks into the man because the man gave no regards to Gregory's personal space.

"What the H..." Gregory started to say before rendered speechless by the sight of the man in white.

"Hello, Gregory. My name is Michael. I am an angel. I have a proposition for you."

Gregory does not reply at first because he couldn't believe what just happened or what he was hearing coming out of this man's mouth. How does he know my name Gregory thought to himself.

Michael waits for a moment for a reply from Gregory. He does not get a reply so he continues to talk to Gregory.

"Gregory there is a war going on between good and evil. God has chosen you to fight in this war. You have to agree to do so because of free will. You can refuse if that is your choice. There is a chance you may lose your life while fighting for the livelihood and betterment of humankind against the demons. I, along with other angels, will train you. You will be a first lieutenant in the human army. The only person you can discuss this with is your mother if you like. She can be your confidant and rock if you need her to be. Will you answer God's call to you?" Michael asked Gregory.

"Ya, yes, yes I will." Gregory finally made himself answer after a long moment of silence.

"Thank you, Gregory. Be at this address tomorrow morning at 7 am." Michael said while giving Gregory a piece of paper with an address on it. Michael disappears as quickly as he appeared leaving Gregory in disbelief and slightly confused. If it were not for the piece of paper in his hand, he would swear that he had imagined the whole thing. Gregory turns to head home. The movie and his friends are no longer occupying his mind or are a priority. The only one he wants to talk to now is the woman who woke him up early that morning, his mother.

It has been almost three days since Jacob went into the old man on the porch. He has not moved night or day. Jacob did not go to the bathroom, eat or sleep. He just sat on the porch with the bugs and elements of the air. Jacob has lost everything and everyone that truly meant something to him. At first, he was very sad and then angry. Now his anger remains with great determination to do any and everything that he can to cause the fall and death of Mistress. He wants to see her suffer little by little by taking away things she desires such as power and domination of everything around her. Pain does not hurt her. She lives for it. However, take away little by little her power, dominance and chance to be the dominator of all would mentally enrage her and tear her playhouse down to the ground. Jacob becomes focused and clear minded. It is time to move on he thought to himself, but before he goes, he has to thank the old man for using his body.

"Thank you for enduring me and my grief for what seemed like a lifetime," he said out loud talking to the old man who could hear him from within the body. "I see that you are wheelchair bound. As a show of my appreciation for your hospitality, I will heal your paralysis. You will be able to walk."

With the thought of his mind, Jacob heals the old man and stands up. It was an easy task for him to do. After all, he is a very powerful ex-second lieutenant demon of Mistress. His powers are strong and can be very dangerous or in this case, very helpful. He walks over to the steps and says "Thank you old man. I will leave you now." With that statement, he leaves the old man's body without even a glance backward. He flies fast over the trees and mountainside. He crosses multiple streams and creeks. On the horizon, he sees the city. It only takes him a few seconds to be in the midst of the hustle and bustle of the roaring city. He needs to find a host. He needs to find someone who has money, power and is in a position of authority. He finds what he is looking for. Trenton McNeil, the owner, and CEO of McNeil Enterprises. He is a Multibillionaire. He enters his body. He loves the skin he is in instantly. He is six foot three, dark brown well-trimmed hair and clean shaved. He has broad shoulders that are accentuated by his tailored made suit. He is on the top floor of the one hundred and twenty story building of the company. Luxury is all around him. He has personal assistants to do his bidding and all the money he needs to make things happen in his favor. He knows everything that his host knows. Therefore, it would be easy for him to acclimate to the life of Trenton McNeil. He called to his assistant via the intercom. He walks in almost immediately.

"Yes Sir," he responded

"Get me a car. I have to do some errands," he ordered.

"Yes, Sir." responded the assistant. The assistant leaves the room as quickly as he came in. Jacob walks over to the coat rack and takes a black trench coat and umbrella off it. He rushes out the door to the elevators. Jacob did not use his private elevators, which Trenton always used. He makes a quick mental note as he pushes the elevator button to use his private elevator in the future, so everything remains status quo. The black Mercedes is waiting downstairs with a driver standing in the rain under an umbrella by the back door waiting to let him in.

"Good morning Tom," Jacob said to the driver.

"Good morning Sir," he replied as he opens the door and closes it once Jacob gets inside the car.

Once in the car, the driver waits for Jacob's orders.

"516 North Fowler Street please Tom," he ordered.

"Yes, Sir," Tom replied as he drives off into the madness of city traffic.

Jacob is going to see Auroa and the Archangel Michael. He knows it would be dangerous. He knows he could lose his life instantly by going before the Archangel Michael. However, desperate times cause for drastic measures. It is a chance he is willing to take. It is a chance he has to take.

Gabe walks into the room with his mind filled with thoughts of what he is going to do to Jackie and John for their failures last night. They had only one task, and they could not accomplish that. He was clear with his orders, very clear. John and Jackie were tasked to bring the barrels of blood from the mass killings that were stored in the west chamber to the ritual room last night. The barrels contained two third of the blood from the bodies of the last two mass murder crime scenes. They took their time delivering the barrels to the ritual room. They barely made it there on time with the blood. The blood had to be here by 2:00 am. Gabe ordered them to have the barrels lined along the altar from wall to the podium by midnight. Those two jackasses failed to follow orders a second time Gabe thought to himself as he walks towards the altar and blood filled barrels. Gabe does not give second chances usually, yet along a third one. Rest assured, there will not be a third chance thought Gabe as he opens the ritual book to the spell that is needed to kick-start the war.

"Cutting it close are we?" Mistress asked as she entered the room wearing her favorite color, purple.

"Yes Mistress," Gabe replied. "Rest assure Mistress, they will pay dearly for falling short of following my orders." Gabe continued to explain his disappointment.

"I'm sure they will. I'm sure they will." Mistress said with a smirk on her face as she looks at the spell in the ritual book to ensure it is the right one. "Five mass killings for five battles. Everything we do from this point on Gabe has to follow protocol to the letter, or we risk forfeiting not only the battles but the overall war. Lucifer, as well as I, would not stand for that. Make sure there are no mistakes, no mishaps, no slipups, or fuckups, hence Azasar. He is your pet project. Make this run smoothly without hiccups. Do I make myself clear?" Mistress asked.

"Yes Mistress, very clear," Gabe answered bowing his head. "Mistress Azasar is not a fuckup. He made a grave mistake, yes, but fuckup he is not." he went out on a limb to say to Mistress

 partly because he knows Azasar is loyal, not only to her but to him as well. He made a big mistake and Mistress is not forgiving in the least. It is not part of her makeup.

"I know he is not a fuckup normally Gabe, but that does not erase the fact that he did fuckup and I mean fuckup royally," she said through clenched teeth at the end of her statement.

Mistress feels herself getting upset. Gabe senses it too. Mistress takes a couple of long deep breaths and Gabe instinctively and wisely changes the subject.

"Mistress, will the ritual follow the same protocol as the last two rituals of before?"

"No, this one is different. The other two mass murder rituals were to obtain the key or permission for war sort to speak. This ritual is to unlock the door of war itself. This ritual will kick-start the whole process. See Gabe up until this point everything could have been stopped. After this ritual is completed, there is no stopping, no take backs and no I want outs. No handsome, this ritual will not follow the same protocol. This ritual will kill everyone in the room save myself and Lucifer. That is why you can't be in the room this time. Please send Azasar in." Mistress said with a light chuckle. "Just kidding. He will not be allowed in the room as well. However, I will need ten assistants in the room with me. I'll leave it up to you to choose them. You have a half an hour before we begin. It will be an excruciating death for them."

Gabe instantly knows he only has to choose eight. He already has two assistants front and center, John and Jackie. How fitting he thought to himself with a smile on his face as he walks eagerly out of the room down to pick and choose the other eight condemn to death demons. How fitting indeed.

Samuel is recharged after only sleeping five hours. A couple of days ago he had a conversation with Father Hannigan that really left his nerves rattled down to the core. Usually, it is an uplifting spiritual moment to spend time with Father Hannigan. He is not only an inspiration to Samuel; he is like a second father. He was there for him in the most trying time of his life when his father died. If it were not for Father Hannigan, Samuel would have gone down the wrong path in life. He started hanging with the wrong crowd. Samuel stopped going to school and became rebellious against his mother. He did not know how to deal with his pain. Therefore, Samuel dealt with it the only way he knew how to. He acted out. It was indeed the darkest moment in his life until a man filled with great light lit up all the corners of his mind and heart. Father Hannigan took the time to reach out to him to pull him out of the darkness and back into the light. For that, he will always be grateful and feel great love for Father Hannigan. He trusts Father Hannigan and knows that he would not lie to him. That is why the story that Father Hannigan told him rattled him so. He is surprised that he was able to sleep not only five hours, but even an hour. Sleep has been so evasive the last couple of days since he learned what he did from Father Hannigan. The hardest part about what Father Hannigan told him is that he cannot talk to anyone about it. They would not believe him anyway. They would think that he had gone mad and have him committed. After seeing what he did in the parking garage a couple of days ago, he went to confide in Father Hannigan. He needed to talk to someone who would not judge him or think that he was losing his mind. He knew that the only person that would believe him would be Father Hannigan. Not even his mother would understand as Father Hannigan would. After telling Father Hannigan about what he saw and felt in the parking garage, The Father took a deep breath before speaking as if getting ready to go underwater for a long period of time.

"Samuel you have known me for a long time. I feel that not only have I been your rock and confidant through some hard periods in your life, but I have also become your friend as well. I know you trust me as I trust you. I am about to tell you something that would require you to have an open mind even to begin to comprehend and believe what I am about to tell you." Father Hannigan starts to shift a little in his seat but steadies himself.

Samuel did not interrupt or pay attention to the Father's apparent uncomfortable body gestures. He wanted to hear what the Father had to say. He wanted to hear the Father say he was not mad or gone completely crazy. He did make a quick mental note that the Father had not changed that much over the years. His dark brown hair is now salt and pepper with the same haircut that the Father wore years ago. He still has that look of authority and yet compassion about him. Father Hannigan stands six foot two with an athletic body, which is not what some people expect of a priest. He never understood why some people always said to him that Father Hannigan does not look like they expected him to look. How does a priest suppose to look Samuel always thought when they said that to him. The ladies always would say he is so handsome like Samuel could relate to their comments. The last thing on his mind or what he wanted to talk about was how handsome Father Hannigan was with them.

Father continues "There is a war going on between good and evil. I know we always tell everyone that, but there is actually a physical, psychological and emotional war going on between good and evil. It is between angels, demons and human fighters. Some humans fight for good, while some fight for evil. Some of the humans will change sides before the fighting is over. Needless to say, I am one of the humans fighting for the good side. I am one of the first lieutenants. Believe it or not you, you have a role to play in this as well. I had to wait until you came to me. I had to wait until the enemy tried to contact you, which is what happened in the parking garage. That was a demon that you saw taunting you. It was trying to gauge your reaction to it, feel you out sort of speak. It wanted to see what kind of reaction you would have to supernatural things. How your mind would handle seeing what you saw. Soon the demon would try to recruit you to their side. Once they determine that you will not fight for them or with them, they may try to kill you." Father Hannigan pauses a brief moment to let what he said to Samuel sink in a bit. After a few minutes, he continues "There are Archangels and angels on Earth now to help guide us and train the human fighters for the battles against the demons."

For the first time, Samuel asked questions. "Why don't the angels fight the battle? Why don't they kill all the demons? Surely they can kill them just as easily as to look at them."

"Yes they can, but this battle has to be primarily fought by the humans. The angels are there to guide the humans in battle. They will even fight alongside them at times, but the choice to suppress evil has to be by the humans. Humans have always been given a choice to choose good over evil." Father Hannigan explained.

Samuel knew too well the kind of choices humans make when tempted with things and desires they want. He has arrested so many people in cases that are the results of human choices. He would often say or think at a crime scene, when will humans be human to other humans?

"Samuel, you will play a part in the battles ahead of us. I didn't want to tell you until the time was right. The angels said that you would be one of the first lieutenants. They have already made contact with the other first lieutenants. They wanted to wait until you were ready to be receptive to the idea and knowledge of what's to come. Samuel, God has chosen you to be one of his fighters against evil. I know that you are worthy of such an appointment. I know that God has chosen the right person. Now I need you to believe it also."

Samuel sat in silence looking at the Father without blinking for a moment. He cleared his throat before he replied to the Father.

"Father, what do I have to do?" he asked in a broken voice.

"God's will Samuel. God's will." Father Hannigan replied.

"I will set up a meeting with you and the Archangel Michael," he informed Samuel.

"The Archangel Michael?" Samuel asked in disbelief.

He never thought he would ever meet the Archangel Michael in real life. He had studied about the angels so much when he was growing up. His favorite has always been the Archangel Michael, who is the most powerful one of them all. The one who defeated Satan. Samuel felt blessed and privileged to be chosen by God to fight on his behalf against evil. It touched his heart and soul that God's grace shines down on him. Tears well up in his eyes and roll down his cheeks. Father understood what the tears meant without saying a word. They sat in silence for a while before Samuel got up, hugged Father Hannigan and went home to try to sleep, which he was surprised that he was able to do so after what Father Hannigan told him. It was still hard for his mind to grasp the reality of it all. However, after the things he has seen after leaving Father Hannigan these past few days, he is entirely convinced. Once he got home after leaving Father Hannigan, he tried to close his eyes to sleep. He turned over to his side in bed and opened his eyes to see the same man from the parking garage sitting in a chair in his room looking at him. Startled, he sat up and turned on the lamp, and no one was there. Another time he was on his way to investigate multiple homicides. While he was speeding through traffic, he looked in his rearview mirror, and the same man was sitting in the back seat of his car.

He said, "Hello Samuel."

Samuel almost lost control of the vehicle before coming to a complete stop. When he looked in the back seat after stopping the car, the man had disappeared. It took a while for Samuel to calm down after seeing that. Once he got to the crime scene, multiple officers kept asking him if he was alright. His FBI unit that he is in charge of is beginning to show concern for him and his lack of sleep. Samuel had to give himself a pep talk to fix his behavior and how he was carrying himself. The last thing he needs is for the men and women who he leads to doubt his abilities in leading them and making competent professional decisions concerning the multiple murder cases, especially the ones with the sixty-four bodies that were found two weeks apart from each other.

The two weeks mark after the last sixty-four bodies were found in the hotel room will be here in a little over a week. Samuel could not help but wonder if there would be another discovery of mass killings soon. Something inside him made him feel that the murders were connected to the conversation with Father Hannigan.

The day before yesterday Samuel was shaving in his bathroom. Nothing was out of the ordinary. The same routine he had done countless of times before. Something did not look right in the mirror to him. It was like his reflection had a delay reaction to all the things that he was doing. It was not synchronized to his movements. Samuel stopped shaving. His reflection stopped shaving a few seconds later. He leaned in towards the mirror. His reflection did the same thing a few seconds later. His reflection had a smirk on its face and reached out the mirror and grabbed him. Samuel was paralyzed with fear at first. He could not believe his eyes.

"Come join us Samuel!" his reflection yelled out at him while holding him by his shoulders.

Samuel struggled for a moment and freed himself from the reflection's grasp. He leaned back against the shower door gasping for air. When he looked in the mirror, all was normal and in synch. The demon was gone. All that remained of the horrifying moment was the rapid beating of his heart and his heavy breathing. He knew he was not losing his mind. If it weren't for the conversation he had with Father Hannigan, he would swear he was losing his mind. After a few minutes, he calmed down enough to finish shaving from across the room. He did not have enough nerve to stand close to the mirror anytime soon. He used the water from the shower to finish shaving. Father Hannigan had told him that the demons would be coming after him to recruit him. If they are unable to do so, they may try to kill him. He was not willing to take a chance in the same spot twice.

He will get a lot of answers to his questions about what is going on. Father Hannigan and Michael have set up a meeting with him, the other lieutenants, the angels and the leader of the resistance, Auroa. Yes, knowledge is power he thought to himself. It is also capable of sending a person to the point of no return to the way things used to be. A point that not only changes things, but it also changes a person as well.

John and Jackie stand clueless with the other eight demons Gabe had chosen to assist Mistress in her final ritual to kick start the war.

"Gabe it's time for you to leave," Mistress said in a low soft voice while reaching out to touch his face.

Gabe leans into her hand. Her touch weakens his knees. He almost buckles and falls to the floor.

"Yes Mistress," he replied.

He waits until she removes her hand from his face before turning to leave as ordered. He shuts the tall double doors behind him. Mistress turns her attention to making sure everything is in place on the altar for the ritual. She stands in the middle facing the alter while five demons flank each side of her facing the altar as well.

"Do not move from your post. You may be tempted to do so, so I am going to use my powers to make you stay in your position," she informed them.

Then with one word, she locks them into place. "Stay."

They are unable to move even though they are aware of what is going on around them. This ritual will be different from the last ones. Not only will the ten demons die in this ritual, but Lucifer himself will be performing the ceremony. The power that is needed to do this ceremony requires someone with greater power than Mistress, which can only be done by Lucifer himself. No other demon except for Mistress is powerful enough to survive while being in the room with Lucifer when a power of that magnitude is being used. It will almost instantly kill every demon within the four walls. There is great pain and suffering for a short period of time before they die, but die they surely will.

"It's time," Mistress said.

Lucifer is right on time. The ten demons' faces are stricken with fear. They naturally had the will to kneel, but Mistress had locked them into place. They are all afraid to stand in the presence of Lucifer. However, today the proper protocol and courtesy of low ranking demons are far from the mind of Lucifer. He has bigger and better things on his mind, WAR! Lucifer stands on the other side of the massive wooden altar facing Mistress with a display of items needed for the ritual on the altar between them. Some would think that Lucifer would be a hideous beast to look at, but it is quite the opposite. After all, he is a fallen angel. He is beautiful in every way except for inside where his evil is unimaginable. He has no mercy, no tolerance, no understanding, no compassion, no sympathy and no forgiveness. He is ambrosia to the eyes to look at if there was such a thing. He is tall with a muscular yet athletic body. His voice sounds like music in perfect pitch. His dark brown full of body hair flows freely down to his shoulders. His skin looks soft and is tan, but not too dark. His dark brown eyes pierce down into the core being of who his gaze is unfortunately bestowed upon. His presence weakens demons' as well as humans' knees while his gaze crumbles either one to the floor. He doesn't have to state who or what he is no more than a lion has to declare itself a lion. He is pure unadulterated evil in an angelic form of a body. After all, he is the Fallen Angel.

"Hello, Mistress. Let us begin." he greeted her and went straight to the task at hand.

As Lucifer starts the incantation to the ritual, Mistress stands still in silence like all the other demons in the room. His voice sounds like music. His voice is so loud that it shakes the wooden altar. The other demons remain wide-eyed with not only fear of being in Lucifer's presence but fear of the unknown as well. They were not told what to expect. As Lucifer continues to bellow out the words to the ritual, he begins to glow. The blood in the barrels begins to bubble. Excitement grows within Mistress from seeing her Master in such pure form even though she fears him. Her admiration and loyalty are deeply rooted within her. A sense of being proud of Lucifer comes over her. She is his number one. She is his ultimate right hand. She is his General.

All of a sudden the blood rises straight up in the air out of the barrels. The blood comes down upon all the demons lined up at the altar except for Mistress. As the blood baptizes each demon, his or her body develop a red fire glow under the skin all over. All the demons cry out in agony as a result. Lucifer chants louder and faster. Finally, one by one, each of the blood marinated demons stops crying out in pain as their bodies seem to turn from bright red to black, then to ashes and then collapse on the floor in front of the altar. Mistress stands facing Lucifer in silence and awe as he comes to the end of his incantations in his angelic musical voice. Lucifer does not look at the remnants of the fallen demons at the altar. Instead, he holds his gaze with Mistress in silence. After a moment a broad smile comes across both of their faces while maintaining intense eye contact with one another.

"Now go win me a war Mistress," Lucifer said in a commanding voice laced with enthusiasm.

"Win I will Master, win I will," Mistress replied enthusiastically as well.

So much has happened in such a short period Jacob thought to himself. He never thought that he would be in the position that he is in within the war for domination. Jacob never dreamed that he would be fighting against Mistress. He was one of her most loyal servants. She changed all of that. She changed him when she killed his family, his beloved daughter, and wife. We were so loyal to her thought Jacob. I would have died for Mistress, and she repaid my loyalty by killing my family. Jacob's thoughts have only one steadfast thought, kill Mistress by any means necessary. That meant that he would do whatever it takes to accomplish the task, even meeting face to face with an Archangel. He knows that every encounter in the past between a demon and an Archangel had ended with the death of the demon, no exceptions. He has lost it all except his life. Now he is more than willing to risk losing that if it means having a chance to kill Mistress.

The last couple of days can attest to how far he is willing to go to killing Mistress. A couple of days ago his driver took him to 516 North Fowler Street. Once there, he sat out in the car with his driver for about an hour waiting for the right person to come along who would be very receptive to his will. He knew he could not just walk up the stairs and knock on the door. The Archangel would incinerate him before he could say one word. Finally, a young boy who appeared to be homeless walked towards the car. Jacob got out of the car and walked over to the boy who looked about ten or twelve years old. He was dressed in blue jeans, a dirt-stained used to be white tee shirt, and a flannel long sleeve shirt. It was odd that the kid did not have on a coat in this cold weather. His shoes did not have shoe strings in them. His face was dirty, and his hair was greasy and unkempt.

"Hey, kid how would you like to make a thousand dollars?" Jacob asked the boy who looked like and smelled like he had not had a bath in days.

"Mister, I am not into that." the boy snapped back with a disgusted look on his face.

"No kid, you got it all wrong. I just want you to deliver a message for me to apartment twenty-six in this building. I'll give you one thousand dollars."

"What's the catch?" the kid asked suspiciously.

"No catch. Deliver this note to Michael in room twenty-six, and I'll pay you a thousand dollars when you come back down." Jacob reassured him.

The kid looked at Jacob for a moment sizing him up and trying to read if he was on the up and up. Finally, he asked, "Where is the note?"

The boy was holding out a hand with five dirty fingernails. Jacob gave him a note he had written in the car while waiting for the perfect messenger to come along. The note had explained who he was, the events that had transpired, his willingness to help aid the good side in the fight against Mistress and his desire to meet face to face with Michael and the leader of them. He gave the boy the note.

"You better have my money when I come back." the boy said to Jacob with an uncanny authority for a kid his age.

He turned and walked towards the building. Jacob was nervous for the first time in centuries. He did not know what to expect. The Archangel could appear before him in a blink of an eye and smite him to ashes without giving him a chance to speak. The kid came out of the building. He walked over to Jacob and held out his dirty right hand.

"It's delivered," he said to Jacob.

"You gave it to a man name..." Jacob started to ask.

"Yeah, yeah, yeah, I gave it to Michael." the kid cut him off.

He wanted his money, not conversation. Jacob took out his wallet and counted ten one hundred crisp dollar bills. He handed it to the kid. Before Jacob could say thank you, the kid turned and ran in the other direction away from him. It was as if he thought Jacob would take the money back or something. Jacob turned to look at the apartment building, but he looked into the face of the Archangel Michael instead. He was less than two feet in front of him. Instant fear filled his being. He was paralyzed with it.

"Hello, Jacob." Michael greeted him with an intensely stern look on his face. After a moment that seemed like an eternity to Jacob, he finally found his voice and replied "Hello Michael."

"Relax, if I wanted you dead, you would be by now," he informed Jacob.

"I know," Jacob replied.

"Shall we talk?" Michael asked.

"Yes, I would like that very much," Jacob replied.

Michael stepped closer to Jacob. Jacob became nervous again. Michael wanted Jacob to heed the gravity of his words.

"Jacob you know who I am. You know that this is a very rare situation that we both find ourselves in. If you show any signs of deception, I will not hesitate to kill you. No questions asked. Do we understand each other?" Michael asked him and waited for his reply.

"Yes, yes we understand each other," Jacob answered nervously.

The Archangel was too close to him for his comfort.

"You have requested an audience with myself and the leader of the human resistance. An audience you should have." Michael held out his hand and gestured for him to go inside the building. Jacob accepted the invitation. Michael did not trust Jacob. Therefore, he enclosed Auroa in an invisible angel protection case that no demonic power could get through to harm her. Michael did not have to worry about himself. He knew that the demon could not hurt him. Of course, Jacob knew he was powerless against the Archangel as well. That is the part that made him so nervous. Jacob was very nervous being so close to the Archangel. In all his time of existence, he had never felt such anxiety and fear as he did that day.

Michael was calm. After all, he had nothing to fear. The demon did not have the power to harm him, and Auroa was safe behind an invisible shield that he had enclosed her in. The only one who was in the hot seat was Jacob. Michael had thought to himself that he would not hesitate to kill Jacob in a blink of an eye if he looked like he was about to step out of line. The only reason Michael was entertaining Jacob was that he felt that the humans need any advantage or information they can get. Any helpful information, even from a demon, would be welcomed. Michael had to remain neutral. He could not let his dislikes for demons get in the way of accepting information that could help the humans in the long run in their fight against Mistress and her army of demons as well as her human followers. Uriel and

Gabriel were waiting in the room with Auroa when Jacob and Michael walked into the room. Suddenly Jacob had the strong urge to run for cover. He did not expect to see the other two Archangels as well. Then again he should have expected as much because he is taking an audience with the leader of the human fighters Jacob had thought to himself.

Gabriel and Uriel were standing flanking Auroa who was sitting in a high armed leather chair against the far wall of the room. The chair did look a little big for her even though she is not a small framed female. Gabriel and Uriel were dressed in all white just like Michael. Gabriel's blonde shoulder length wavy hair was like the sun around the perfect fair complexion of his face. His dark blue eyes stared intently at Jacob. Jacob felt as though Gabriel was looking straight through him. What Jacob didn't know was that Gabriel was looking through him in a sense. Gabriel could see the real face of the demon within the human host. He saw Jacob's true form for what he is, a demon with his own unique appearance. Gabriel saw the brown and green scaly body with the six four-inch horns on his head. Also, he could see the violet colored eyes, uneven, jagged sharp teeth, and jet black shiny wings.

Gabriel instantly wanted to kill him, but their leader, Michael had given him safe passage for the moment and ordered for him not to be harmed. Before in the past, Gabriel would have been immutable to such an idea of entertaining an audience with Jacob. However, over the millenniums, Michael had changed Gabriel's point of views and war tactics that enabled him to contain himself from ripping this demon apart on sight. Gabriel was a scary sight to Jacob. However, Uriel is only second to Michael when it comes to being foreboding to Jacob. Uriel's dark brown skin color is a beautiful contrast to the white attire he was wearing. His black dreadlocks drape over his shoulders and down to his mid-back. The front locks were pulled back and bound so not to drape over his face. Uriel strong, intense overbearing stare almost made Jacob's knees buckle. Jacob had to look away from Uriel to remain standing. Michael gestured for Jacob to sit in a wooden dining room table chair directly in front of Gabriel, Uriel, and Auroa. Michael positioned himself in front of Jacob next to Gabriel. There was a reason Michael stood near Gabriel. Even though he had great confidence that Gabriel had every intention of following his order not to harm Jacob, He knew if Jacob shows any deception or steps out of line minutely, Gabriel may react in an instant trying to kill him due to instinct.

"So tell us why you risk life and limb to talk to us," Michael said to Jacob.

Jacob told them about all that had transpired up to that point. He informed them of his intentions to do whatever it takes to bring Mistress's life to an end. Jacob vowed to help them with intelligence, service, identification of demons and humans fighting for the side of Mistress and even help in the fight itself against Mistress. He informed them that he was a second lieutenant in the army of Mistress. He was privy to top secret and beyond information, fighting tactics and future projects as well as current projects that Mistress had in place already.

The angels and Auroa listen to Jacob without interrupting him. Once it appeared that Jacob had finished talking, Michael was first to speak.

"Jacob we do seem to be at an impasse. Either we take a chance and trust you at face value, or we determine that you're not worth the risk and kill you where you sit."

Jacob becomes paralyzed with fear. He stops breathing, even though he did not need it to survive. Even if he wants to make a sound, nothing will come out of his mouth anyway. Michael looks at Auroa.

"You are the leader of this army. It is time you make your first difficult decision. What do you want to do?" Michael asked Auroa.

Auroa is caught off guard. She didn't know how to reply to such a question. She definitely did not think she is competent enough to make a sound decision concerning the matter at hand. No one spoke. They seemed very patient while waiting for Auroa to respond. She cleared her throat.

"Do you see or feel any deception in him or in what he has told us thus far?" she asked Michael.

"No, we have not detected any deception so far Auroa," Michael answered her.

"Okay. Would we have a great advantage having Jacob on our side?" she asked another vital question.

"Yes, we would," Michael informed her.

"Then welcome to the good side Jacob," she spoke for the first time directly to Jacob.

Jacob finally took in a breath of air.

"Thank you," he replied in almost a whisper to Auroa.

Michael walked slowly towards Jacob closing the distance between the two of them.

"Don't disappoint us in any way and you will be given a safe passage as well as allowed to live. If you do try to betray us in any way, death would be something that you would beg for in the end." Michael warned Jacob

"All I want is to see Mistress fall from power and die," Jacob replied.

"Then see you will," Michael informed him. "See you will." He repeated himself.

Auroa sits quietly while watching Michael train the small band of fighters who had been waiting impatiently for him to finish training the previous group of soldiers. Michael is working with the smallest in the group at this time, T'Ariel, who is short and petite. Michael is trying to show her how to use her weight to throw her opponent who she may be fighting one day. T'Ariel pays close attention to Michael's techniques. She mimics Michaels's moves perfectly. Michael is astonished at how quickly she catches on.

The side gate opens with a squeak. Gregory walks into the backyard for the first time. T'Ariel stops in mid-technique and stares at Gregory as he glides gracefully down the hill towards the group of fighters being trained. His swagger is definitely his own. T'Ariel has stopped breathing for a moment. She remembers to start breathing again when Gregory looks over at Michael and says "I'm sorry I am late. I had to do something for my Mom."

Gregory's voice was deep, manly and smooth. He doesn't even glance at T'Ariel. He is focused on the task at hand, training and being the best he can be in battle.

"It's okay Gregory. We just started," Michael replied. "Everyone this is Gregory. He is a new addition to our team. Please introduce yourself when you get a chance," Michael said while introducing Gregory to all the fighters in the yard. "Gregory this is Auroa, the leader of the humans. Auroa this is Gregory," said Michael.

"Hello, Gregory. Welcome to our team." Auroa said with a welcoming smile.

"Thank you for having me," Gregory replied back with a broad smile.

Before Michael could turn around and continue to teach T'Ariel more fighting techniques, she darts over to Gregory and introduces herself. "Hello, my name is T'Ariel," she said while holding out her right hand to shake his.

Gregory reaches out his right hand and shakes hers. "Hello, nice to meet you," he said with a smile. He is not thinking of her like she is thinking of him. His mind is on the cause that he was called to fight. However, from the first moment T'Ariel laid eyes on Gregory, she wanted to know him as well as belong to each other. She does not care that she could not explain the intense attraction. All she knows is that Gregory had her from the moment he walked through the squeaky iron gate. The moment he opened the gate, he opened her heart to him as well.

"Claudia go and do as you're told." Mistress dismisses her with authority.

Claudia gets up and walks quietly out of the room. She feels a tinge of excitement as she pushes open the large iron and wooden door to exit the mansion. She walks slowly to her black Lexus parked to the far left of the large circular driveway. She wants to please Mistress in any and every way. It not only took her hundreds of years for her to reach the level that she is currently in the organization but also it took a long time for her to reach the level that she is at in Mistress's eyes as well. There is no sleeping your way up the ranks with Mistress. Claudia worked hard long hours many days and years to achieve the status and reputation that she has now. The second lieutenant takes a lot of dedication and attention to detail not only to achieve but to maintain in an army of Mistress. Claudia does not need a family with a husband and children because she is married to her job and her ambition to succeed. Claudia drives for hours to reach the nearby city. The mansion is indeed out in the boonies. Of course, Claudia does not need a car to travel at almost the speed of light from place to place, but Claudia was not in a hurry. After all, she is two thousand four hundred and fifty-six years old. A couple of hours to her is not even equivalent to a second to an old human. The city is alive as usual. Unlike the county living that surrounds the mansion, the city never sleeps. Claudia exits the freeway and heads up to the west side of the town towards the parking garage that she likes to park her vehicle while she roams about the city on foot, in the air or even at the speed of light.

"Hello, Miss Claudia. How are you doing tonight?" the gate guard to the parking garage asked Claudia.

"I'm doing good George. How are you doing tonight?" Claudia asked with a broad smile.

"I'm still alive and making the donuts," George responded as he gives her a ticket and pushes the button for her to go through the gate. Claudia drives slowly up the winding drive to the top level where she always likes to park. Claudia makes a mental note of the fact that she would have to give up her toy, her playmate, but Mistress orders were very cut and dry. Mistress made a point to make the orders crystal clear. She did not want Claudia to be distracted during the war.

How wonderful it has been though to torture Anya so. She smiles to herself as she thinks about the first encounter she had with Anya. She chose her because Anya was a typical high school bully. Also, there was another reason she chose Anya that she will reveal in time to Anya when the time is right. The prettiest girl in the school who always got what she wanted and never had to earn her way. That is what Claudia hates the most about Anya. Anya never had to earn her way. She is not only Daddy's and Mommy's little girl, but she is everybody's little girl except the people she steps on, belittles or treats as dirt beneath her feet. It gave Claudia great pleasure to torture Anya to reduce her to a whimpering idiot at times. Claudia relished in the pleasure to cause her to have an uncontrollable outburst in the middle of a quiet classroom. A great pleasure indeed Claudia thought to herself as a broad smile spreads across her face. She will leave the car and the human host body here in the car on the top level of the parking garage. She is going to put the human host to sleep with the sheer will of her mind while she is gone.

The human within the host body is not a very strong-willed human. She does not fight as others had done so in the past. Over Claudia's hundreds of years in existence, she has had thousands of hosts. Some so fierce that it made it not only unbearable for Claudia to occupy their bodies, but impossible for long periods of time as well. No, this host is nice, and comfy Claudia thought to herself as she whispers to her host "I'll be back. Sleep baby girl. Sleep."

Claudia could tell that the human lost consciousness. As the human falls asleep inside, Claudia slips out of the body and flies in her invisible form into the air. As she did, she wonders what her pet was doing now. Claudia has been torturing Anya for almost two years. Claudia smirks as she thought to herself that Anya is not abusing anyone tonight.

"No, you're my bitch," Claudia said out loud as she made it to the front door of Anya's house.

Anya is in her room as she is most of the time these days. She is scared to come out and play thought Claudia. Claudia wants to take her time. Mistress gave her seventy-two hours to get rid of her toy and not a minute longer. There is a lot of perks that Mistress has that comes along with being the oldest and most powerful demon of them all. She can see things within her mind that is happening with almost any demon at any given time just by thinking of the demon. However, the oldest and mighty demons can shield Mistress's ability to see what they are doing at present. They record with their mind so Mistress can see what has taken place later when they are back in her presence. Some old demons have the same ability like Mistress to see what a few demons under their command or demons who are slaves to them are doing at any given time, but not able to see with almost all the demons as Mistress does. Therefore, there is no fooling or tricking Mistress into thinking that Anya is dead or released from being a pet. Mistress would know, and it would cost Claudia not only her job, but her life as well for lying or trying to deceive Mistress.

Claudia enters in her invisible form through the front door without opening it. She did not go immediately up to Anya's room. Instead, she takes a nice stroll around the first floor of the lavished home. This house is too big for three people. Anya is the only child, and a very undeserving spoiled one at that thought Claudia. Tonight both parents are at home. So often, even during her current turmoil of existence, her mother and father spent a lot of time away from the house in the arms of their lovers. Their marriage was over a long time ago. They stay together because it is comfortable financially. They do not even put Anya in the equation when determining to stay together. Each one of them, Mom, Dad, and Anya are selfish. Well within seventy-two hours their lives will change, well at least two of them Claudia thought to herself. One of their lives will end altogether. The Mother is in the family room secretly texting her lover, and the Father is in the living room professing his love to his Mistress via text as well. Each knows the other has someone else but chooses to turn a blind eye to the fact to continue to live the lifestyle they are accustom to living. Greed, lust, and selfishness are trademarks of this broken intact family. I will break you even more thought Claudia as she walks invisibly to the foot of the stairs. Claudia smiles as she says to herself that she will give the parents, not Anya, a few more peaceful nights. Not only would sunlight be on the horizon within a few days from now, but a diabolical child of Hell will accompany it, and her name is Claudia.

This meeting is going to be a very important meeting today. Michael has arranged a meeting with Father Hannigan, all the angels, Auroa, all the lieutenants, Samuel and even Jacob. It is time for all the main leaders in this fight meet each other and get an overview of what is going on as well as what is to come in time. Traffic is mad this time of morning Michael thought to himself as he drives Auroa to Father Hannigan's church. Auroa sits in silence in the passenger seat staring out the window. He asked her earlier if she had any questions or was nervous. She said no to both questions. He does not feel he needs to ask her again. She has come a long way the past few weeks in accepting her role as the leader as well as the events that seem just to keep unfolding before her like a Rolodex. Each time she seemed to rise to the occasion and handled every event well. However, Michael knows these small events have no bearing on the major events and decisions making that she will have to endure, master, live through and make in the long run. He prays every day that she will be strong enough to make the right decision when the time comes that would keep her on the good side of the fight.

Not only is the traffic bad, but the rainy weather also does not help matters either. These drivers need to all be herded in a field and ordered to watch as all their cars are set on fire due to not being used properly thought Michael as a yellow cab cuts in front of him even though it did not have enough room to do so beforehand.

The only ones who are already at the church are the angels and Father Hannigan. When Michael and Auroa walk into the church, they are all standing at the front of the church. Michael and Auroa walk up the aisle at a nice slow pace. He purposely slows himself to ensure he maintains his stride beside her. Once they get to the front of the church, Michael walks over to Father Hannigan who smiles and bows his head.

"Hello, Michael." Father Hannigan said.

"Hello, Father. This is Auroa, the leader of the human fighters. Auroa, this is Father Hannigan. He is a true servant of God." he introduced the two of them.

"Hello, Auroa. It is a pleasure to meet you finally." Father Hannigan said to Auroa.

"Hello, Father. It is nice to meet you as well." Auroa said in a soft feminine voice.

The Father smiles at her. She is way more than he expected. He could tell she is strong and has the atmosphere of a leader.

"You will do well," he said to her.

"Thank you, Father," she replied.

"You are very welcome my child," Father replied.

Jacob walks through the door. Father Hannigan looks up and recognizes him instantly from the description that Michael had given him earlier. Jacob walks up to the front of the church.

"Jacob this is Father Hannigan." Michael introduced him to the Father.

"Hello, Father." Jacob greeted him while maintaining eye contact.

"Hello, Jacob. Welcome aboard." the father replied.

He is not prejudiced against the demon. He sees the big picture of this war and welcomes whatever help comes their way. Jacob could feel the acceptance. Michael has honestly kept his word and given him a safe passage. All trust his judgment. From that moment on Jacob silently vows that he would not let him down or he would die trying. Loyalty has always been a strong trait of Jacob. Once he commits to something or someone, he would give it all to not let the person or being down. Again he would accomplish the task or die trying.

The first of the three hundred first, second and third lieutenants start to filter into the church. These few are early. They have about thirty more minutes before Michael starts speaking. Jacob looks around the enormous, massive church. It could comfortably hold five hundred or more people. The dark mahogany wood pews and trimmings are beautifully contrasted with the burgundy and gold cloths, seats and carpet. The statues of the saints that line the walls flanking the pews give an angelic like atmosphere inside the church. This building is beautiful and gives off a sense of tranquility Jacob thought to himself. Maybe this is why they come here to worship instead of going to any of the other umpteen catholic churches in this area.

Usually, Jacob would not be able to enter this holy place. However, Michael has used his limitless strong beyond imagination power and granted him access to the church. Jacob is not so nervous as he had been when he first met the Archangel. As the time passes, he realizes that Michael is not only true to his word but a good leader as well. It takes a strong leader to put aside his or her personal feelings and do what is in the best interest of the team as a whole. Jacob feels that he is on the right side of the fence in this war. He feels he would follow Michael anywhere. This is a rare situation that both he and Michael find themselves in. Something like this only happens every few millenniums where an angel and a demon are fighting on the same side.

Jacob thoughts are interrupted by the main door of the church opening and closing. The lieutenants are starting to funnel into the church. So many of them thought Jacob. The lieutenants will brief the foot soldiers later. All of them could not fit into the church. Not all of the lieutenants know who Jacob is. That will be revealed today by Michael. At first, Jacob was apprehensive about telling everyone. However, Michael reassured him that all would be fine. Also, he said that the fighters have a right to know who is standing beside them in the trenches while they are risking their lives. Michael reminded Jacob that he would be risking his own life as well. Jacob never thought of it that way until Michael pointed it out. It never occurred to him that while he is fighting against Mistress, he will be risking his very existence to do so. Maybe because it never really mattered since all he can think of is destroying Mistress and everything she has built or hope to build. He has been tunnel vision.

As the pews began to fill, the angels and Auroa line up in the front of the church facing the crowd. Michael stands at the right of Auroa. He beckons for Jacob to join him and stand on the left side of Auroa. This is a very significant gesture. It means that Michael trusts Jacob by allowing him to stand so close to Auroa. It says that he is a vital part of the team as well. Loyalty is what compels Jacob. It is one of the reasons he is standing on this side of the fight instead of Mistress side of the battle. He was very loyal to his wife and daughter who Mistress snuffed out their life light like a strong wind blows out a candle. Jacob does not put much hope that he will survive this war. All he wants to do is to be there when Mistress dies, and her world falls to ruins.

Then he would happily go into the unknown nothing to follow his wife and daughter. After all, he would have nothing else to live for anyway.

The last few lieutenants enter the church. Michael begins to speak, and all fall silent. His voice is loud and could be heard throughout the church clearly. He introduces Auroa, the angels, and Jacob to everyone. He informs everyone of what Jacob is and his purpose for being here today. Also, he tells them that Jacob is on their side and the angels have given him a safe passage. Under no circumstance is that safe passage to be violated by anyone, human or angel. Afterward, Michael takes a deep breath and addresses the crowd in a more solemn tone.

"The battles ahead will be of grave danger and perilous. I won't lie to you. Not all will make it to the final battle. Your victory, in the end, is depending on your determination, your ferocity, your will to fight until the very end for good against evil with all your might, heart and soul as well as your unyielding steadfast belief that God wills you and empowers you. There will be five battles as well as many confrontations with the demons, some small and some great. There will be many loses, some great and some small. However, if you keep your eye on the horizon on the prize of human salvation and the will of God, you all will prevail. You will win this fight. You will be victorious." Michael pauses for a moment then continues. "There are things that we must do and prevent first before the final battle can be fought. We must find and lay claim to at least six of ten relics. A relic could be a single item or a group of items to equal one category of a relic. These relics allow us to have the power we will need to kill the head demon who is called Mistress in the end. If you ask her what her name is, she would reply, "I am who I am." she is the oldest and most powerful demon. The combined power of the relics would ensure her defeat. We only need six of them to have a chance at killing her. She has her Army out looking for relics as well. We have two relics already. The demons do not have any at this time. Don't let the fact that we already have two relics make you complacent, so you let down your guard and feel like we don't have to give this fight all we got. I must impress upon you all the gravity of the situation, which would be catastrophic and cataclysmic if she should obtain five relics. If Mistress obtains five relics, we would be unable to obtain six relics, which means we would not be able to destroy or defeat her. Her darkness, pain, and suffering would engulf the Earth as well as humankind. Suffering and death will fall to all who are not needed as a human host for the demons. We are all fighting for your very existence and your souls. God has not abandoned you. Don't abandon him." Michael concluded.

He touches Auroa on her shoulder at which time she steps forward two steps and addresses the crowd.

"My fellow comrades so much has changed in such a short period of time. If you had told me a couple of months ago that I would be fighting with angels, a demon and you all against evil demons that want to take over our world and existence, I would have dismissed you as crazy. If you had told me that I would be the leader of the fighters in this war, I would have thought that you are completely mental and ran the other way. Well, the reality of it is I am fighting with angels, a demon and with you all against evil demons that want to take over our world and existence. I am the leader of the fighters in this war. All I ask of you is the same that I will do or not do. I will fight with all my might, heart, soul and being. I will not yield. I will not tire. I will not falter. I will not be deterred. I will not give up. I ask that you follow me and believe in me as I truly believe in you." Auroa looks around the church as the last words leave her lips. She wants to look into every one of their eyes that she could. She believes in these fighters with all her heart and prays that they feel the same about her.

One of them starts to chant Auroa's name. More and more lieutenants join in until the entire crowd, humans, angels, and demon are shouting her name at the top of their voice all at once. Tears of gratitude roll down Auroa's cheeks. Michael and the other angels stand by their leader who they have grown proud of in such a short period. However, deep inside Michael's thoughts are that he prays that Auroa maintains this conviction when it comes time for her to resist the temptation of turning evil. The choice will be hers to make and hers alone.

The two men and two women sit on the floor facing Mistress and Gabe. Gabe sits on the right side of Mistress's feet. The men and women are new hosts to demons who are meeting Mistress for the first time. The demons inside the bodies are very eager to please Mistress in any way she desires or commands. They are naked and have not earned the right to wear clothes in

Mistress's presence yet. Mistress looks at the beauty of them all. The women are a blonde and a redhead. The blonde is petite, while the redhead is voluptuous with beautiful curves. The men are tall. One of them has fair skin over a chiseled muscular body. His broad shoulders are strong and inviting. The other man is not only handsome, but he is also beautiful to look at. His bronze ebony skin glistens over his Nubian king like body of muscles. Mistress looks at them with lust in her eyes. How Mistress loves a tall, strong manly man's body. Once she had her fill of taking in all four as eye candy, she speaks softly with a sense of authority in her voice.

"Mentally you will make my will your will. All you want to do is please me. If I am happy, you are happy. Physically you will be my canvas for my masterpiece of pleasure and pain. I will use your body along with your mind for my pleasure. The things I will do to you and allow you to do to me will be nothing short of a pure erotic pleasure. Visually you would perform for me. You will do things that are pleasing to my eyes. You will even give yourself to others for the mere fact it pleases me to watch. My will is the only will. Therefore, it will be your will. My pleasure is the only pleasure. Therefore, it will be your pleasure to do or say whatever pleases me or gives me pleasure. You will serve only me. You will dominate others, and I will dominate you. Now get on your knees and prepare to please me." she commanded the four sitting on the floor. They all rise to a kneeling position. Before Mistress could lean back and issue her next command, a look of soberness comes over her face.

"Get out all of you! You too Gabe!" she yelled out.

Almost faster than the eye could see, they all ran out of the room in fear, including Gabe. Mistress sits up straight in the chair and waits in silence.

Finally, she says "Yes Master, how can I be of service to you?" she asked in a very low submissive voice.

All of a sudden it was like an invisible hand hits her across the face knocking her out of her chair and into the wall almost twenty feet away. She did not move from where she lay on the floor. She keeps her head down and does not make a sound. Again she is struck by something invisible and thrown across the room. This time she did speak.

"Master please forgive me for letting Jacob escape. He was..."

Before she could finish, she is struck again and again and again until she is unable to speak while lying on the floor breathing heavily. Her bones could be heard breaking with every blow. She heals herself almost instantly, even though the last blow caused her to be a little slower at healing this time.

"Yes, I know it's a great setback to have him on the other side. I will pull it together Master. I will make you proud."

There is only one reply in a loud demonic voice that shook the entire building and mountain.

"You better."

Mistress falls to the floor and coward to her Master who then rips off her clothes, sodomize and rapes her savagely where she lay over and over and over again. She takes it all. She does not dare resist or make a sound. After all, he is Lucifer. He is the Master, and she is the Slave. Her cruelty was taught to her by the Master. Now she is his canvas for pleasure and pain.

T'Ariel works at a nursing home that is filled with ninety-eight percent old people. Only a few young people inhabit the fifteen story facility. She works on the twelfth floor, which is dedicated to psych, Alzheimer's and dementia residents. Tonight instead of being a nurse, she is doing patient care. She is taking care of an old lady who appears to have two personalities inside of her. One second one voice inside of her is cursing someone out while another voice inside of her apologizes to the person she is swearing to and telling her to stop treating the person that way. Other times she has one voice who cries while another voice inside of her consoles her and tells her not to cry. The resident eyes are dark, almost black and piercing in her stare.

T'Ariel had noticed earlier during mealtime that the resident was sitting across the room staring at her on purpose between bites of her food her feeder was giving her. The resident did not break her stare. T'Ariel dismissed it and continued to focus on the person she was feeding. Now it's time for T'Ariel to put the staring resident to bed and wash her. It takes two to put her to bed because she is a hoyer lift resident who does not walk or bear weight to stand. From the time the two caregivers start to hook the resident up to the hoyer to transfer her to bed, the resident verbally abuses both caregivers at first and then T'Ariel lastly because she is left in the room with the resident alone after the transfer.

"I'm going to rip your head off and solve it up your ass." said one voice inside the resident.

"Don't say that." another voice says from the resident. "I will say that. I will say what the hell I please." another voice retorted.

"I didn't say that." another voice said in an apologizing tone of voice.
T"Ariel does not reply to or acknowledge what the resident is saying as she continues to insult T'Ariel relentlessly. It has always made it worse in the past to do so.

"Goodnight," T'Ariel said to the resident as she turns off the dimly lit overhead light.

"Goodnight," replied the resident.

T'Ariel walks over to the resident's roommate and turns on the call light so someone would come and help her transfer the resident to bed. The roommate is sitting in her wheelchair. The charge nurse comes in to assist T'Ariel. "I think Mrs. Jones has two personalities," T'Ariel said to the charge nurse. "It's as if two people are inside of her and talking in a conversation at once," she informed the charge nurse.

"I have noticed that too." said the charge nurse. "There is a nice one and a nasty one." said the charge nurse.

They lift the roommate into bed. The charge nurse leaves the room. T'Ariel goes about her duties of getting the roommate ready for bed. Once she is finished and has cleaned up the area, she turns the roommates overhead light out. The sink and entryway into the room lights are still on. As she is walking out the room, she glances over to Mrs. Jones side of the room. Mrs. Jones is sitting straight up in bed looking at T'Ariel.

"So you think there are two of us inside this wretched old body. There are many in this body, many." Mrs. Jones said in a deep hoarse demon voice. T'Ariel is stun and unable to move or speak in disbelief. "Get out of here you scrawny hag. You're lucky I can't touch you. Very lucky." the demon voice said through laughter as Mrs. Jones body laid back down and closed her eyes. T'Ariel was so shocked at first that she couldn't move.

"Leave!" the demon voice shouted out which scared T'Ariel into motion.

T'Ariel leaves the room. Her heart is beating fast while her heavy breathing makes her look like she just finished sprinting a mile or more.

"Are you okay?" the charge nurse asked her once seeing T'Ariel's condition in the hallway.

"Yes, yes I'm okay." T'Ariel lied.

"Be careful. We can't afford for you to go home too. We are already working short. Also, I don't want you to get hurt. After all, tonight is your last night to work. It would be a shame if you get hurt." said the charge nurse.

"Okay," replied T'Ariel trough heavy breathing. She could not tell anyone what just happened. Not only would they not believe her, but she would come across like she is crazy. Tonight is her last night on the job. She had put in her two weeks notice two weeks ago. She would not be going back into that room alone tonight she thought to herself, that's for sure.

Samuel sits at his desk with a letter in his hand. He had prepared it the night before. It was one of the hardest things he had to write. He has to take a leave of absence from his post with the FBI. He knows it is something that has to be done. He cannot serve two masters. He has to give all his attention to being a first lieutenant in this war. He would not be able to concentrate on solving cases. The leave of absence will be for indefinite. He would probably lose his appointment as lead FBI agent to the Crime Analysis Team, but he knows he has a higher calling to answer to. The stationery used to write his resignation on is nice thought Samuel. He has been sitting at his desk for about an hour talking to himself about what has to be done. Samuel is living his dream. Now he has to give it up for a while. He has a feeling that he may not return. Also, he thinks that he will not be the same after this war. He feels that this job would not be satisfying to him then. He would have outgrown it.

Samuel takes a deep breath, folds up his letter and slides it into an envelope. He does not seal it. He walks over to the hangers and removes his coat. The only stop he makes is to the Director's office before leaving the building. The Director is sitting behind his big oak desk when Samuel enters his office. Samuel explains to the Director his intentions and that he has to take care of some personal things. Because the leave of absence is for indefinite, the Director says that someone else will have to be appointed to his job. A strong tinge of pain gripped Samuel's stomach when he heard that someone else would be appointed to his position. However, the feeling quickly passes. It was as if he almost instantly accepted it as something that has to be done. Something that he has to let go of to move onto what he had to do, be a first lieutenant in the war against evil. It still sounds a little weird even in thought Samuel thought as he let his shoulders relax while coming to terms with his decisions.

Michael has covered things so that the fighters could put all their time and energy as well as minds into the task at hand. Michael is making sure that all their bills are paid, and their families are taken care of in some miracle angel kind of way. Even though Samuel has a good nest egg put away, it is reassuring to know that the people who are fighting next to him in the trenches have their heads in the game. They will not be worried about their bills and the wellbeing of their families. Samuel has a feeling that the battles will be hard enough.

As he walks out of the Director's office, he feels for the first time that beyond a shadow of a doubt he has made the right decision. He feels he has chosen the right path even though it will be dismal and long. It is the right choice in his heart.

Jordan is standing in the doorway of her closet trying to determine what to wear to the dinner party tonight. As usual, Jack is already ready and waiting for her in the other room. She knows he would be walking into the room any minute to tell her to hurry up and get dressed. He would remind her again for the countless amount of times that she always makes them late. Their marriage has grown stronger since Jack's life was spared. They always had a close relationship, but now it's even closer. They can't seem to get enough of each other. They want each other all the time even more so than they did when they first got together as boyfriend and girlfriend. Just like Jordan predicted, Jack opens the door and walks in. He closes it behind him. Jordan lets out a sigh and thinks to herself, here we go. Blah, blah, blah, but to her surprise, Jack does not say anything. Instead, he walks up behind Jordan who is only wearing a bra and panties and hugs her from behind. Jack feels her body heat and the softness of her skin. He softly kisses the back of her neck, tasting her skin as she melts into his touches.

"Mmmm, we are going to be late Jack," she says between moans.

"I don't care," he replies while lowering his kisses down her back and getting on his knees while his hands caress down her body to her panties. He continues to kiss and lick the small of her back. Jack feels his cock get hard in his pants as he pulls down her panties exposing her beautiful round ass. Oh, how he loves her ass he thought. He loves worshiping it. He licks, tastes and nibbles at her ass. Jordan arches her back to give him more access. He spreads her cheeks and buries his mouth and face deep inside between her ass cheeks. Jordan lets out a loud cry of pleasure. Between licks and nibbles, Jack moans as his rock hard cock pulsates in his pants. He loves the feel and taste of her. He stands up and leads her over to the bed. He forcefully bends her over the bed and spreads her legs apart. Jordan buries her face in the comforter to muffle her moans as Jack buries his face in her ass and pussy from behind. She feels so good to him. He wants to drink every drop of her. He loves worshiping her ass and pussy. He shelves his tongue deep inside her pussy feeling the silky wet softness of her. He works his way down to her swollen clit that is fully aroused. She is so hot and wet he thought to himself. His face and mouth are covered with her juices. Jack grabs both of her ass cheeks and pulls them apart. His strong tongue goes deep inside of her ass while his finger finds her G-spot inside her wet hot pussy. As he licks her ass, he massages her G-spot until Jordan explodes passionately with a loud moan. Her tight pussy contracts around his finger while her body convulses on the bed. He stands up and drops his pants to the floor revealing his eight and a half inches of thick rock hard pulsating cock. With one stroke he shoves his cock all the way inside her balls deep. Jordan lets out a loud cry of pain and pleasure as he fills every inch of her pussy with his powerful big cock. He starts stroking her in and out slowly at first deep, hard and slow. Then his rhythm gets faster and faster. She can't contain or control her loud moans of pleasure coming out of her mouth. It feels so damn good. He hurts her so good. Jack loves the way her tight wet pussy grips his cock. He pulls her harder and harder against him, feeling the head of his cock hitting the bottom of her tight wet pussy over and over and over again until he finally explodes deep inside her.

He grips her hips tightly and yells out "Damn Jordan, your pussy is so fucking good!"

His body jerks as the last few drops of cum leaves his cock. His limp body leans over Jordan for a moment while he relaxes and starts breathing normally again. He pulls himself out of her and gets down on his knees. He licks her clean of both of their cum.

Before standing, he leans close to her ear and says "Thank you."

He kisses her neck and leaves her kneeling on the side of the bed with her legs shaking and out of breath. He leaves the room without saying another word.

Michael walks over to the door leading out to the massive backyard of Terrance beautiful estate. It is very nice of Terrance to let some of the fighters practice on his beautiful property Michael thought to himself. He has lost his Fiancé and their home together, but he is still so hopeful for the future as well as for humankind Michael thought as he studies the techniques that the fighters are practicing by themselves this morning before the angels come. He stands in the doorway silently observing them while letting his mind ponder on something that is truly out of the norm for him. Michael has noticed that Terrance goes out of his way to interact with Auroa. He stares a little too long or tries to make her laugh a little too often. Usually, such things would not interest Michael or would go unnoticed by him. However, this time it's different. Michael feels a tinge of jealousy. He hasn't felt such a thing in thousands of years. There is no doubt what he is feeling. Michael is very in tuned with his feelings. It is not his intentions to feel anything for Auroa. The more he fights it, the faster he seems to be falling. So he finally just gave up resisting it, but not acting on it. No one knows, but himself and he wants to keep it that way. Auroa still tries to walk around him half-naked as if he is not the opposite sex or he is her close gay friend. That is so far from the truth thought Michael. After all, his father is full of love and is a jealous God. How could humans believe that he would not possess such emotions he wondered to himself in bewilderment.

He makes a deliberate effort to try to only be around Auroa after she is dressed for the day. However, that is not always full proof. Sometimes after training, she would go back to her room with Michael and start undressing as soon as the door closes behind them. She would be completely naked by the time she makes it to her bathroom door. Most of the time Michael can look away in time. However, there are times he finds it difficult to tear his eyes away from her voluptuous, soft body of curves. Even though Michael is very grateful of all that Terrance is doing to contribute to the success of the humans, he can't help but to want to step in front of him while he is looking at Auroa to ask what are you looking at. He wants to chastise Terrance by saying to him that it's your leader or your superior, but he knows that it doesn't matter. Michael knows he only feels that way because he has feelings for Auroa. If he did not have feelings for her, he would care less about what goes on between the two of them. Even though Michael feels how he feels, he will not let it affect his judgment and treatment of any of the fighters, even Terrance or Auroa herself. He will toe the line. He will make sure that he will not compromise or put Auroa and Terrance in an uncomfortable position. Therefore, his feelings for Auroa will remain a secret to only him. He does feel at times that Uriel picks up on it sometimes, but out of respect and belief in Michael's leadership and judgment, Uriel does not speak words about his observation. He just smiles at Michaels and walks away. All Michael can think to himself when Uriel walks away is that yes Uriel, yes I got it bad. After all, Michael knows that he may have to kill Auroa one day if her choices are not for good or the betterment of humankind. He pushes the thoughts of such a horrible task out of his head for the moment. He will cross that bridge if or when it comes. Hopefully, he never has to drink that cup of tea he says to himself as he walks out into the backyard to the fighters who are happy to see him finally.

They all sit around the oval table. Mistress sits at one end, and Gabe sits at the other to signify the two heads of the table. Azasar along with five other demons, one first lieutenant called Edward, and four other first lieutenants of Mistress occupy the other seats. Mistress looks around the table at the demons that she had summoned earlier while taking a moment to study every one of their faces and body languages before she begins to speak in a low soft voice with a tone of authority.

"I've waited a long time for these days." she began. "The sacrifices of sixty-four bodies times five over a span of sixty-four years have been completed. Now we can begin to move forward to claim our dominion over the Earth. I don't want any mistakes or speed bumps to occur." she said as her glance fell on Azasar.

He shifts in his seat nervously as her eyes fall upon him.

"This time there will be no second chances," she warned while maintaining her eyes focused on Azasar. Everyone knows that not only was she talking to Azasar, but she was also talking to them as well.

The teacher stands at the head of the class giving a lecture and asking random questions about the lesson. She calls at random on different students to answer questions that they should know if they studied the notes that were taken in class days before. Patricia sits in the middle of the first row on the left. She looks like the typical black eight grader. Her hair is braided nice and neat. Her brains are gathered together in a ponytail that drapes down her back midway.

"Patricia what year was the Constitution signed?" the teacher asked.

"Do you want the truth or do you want what the textbook states?" Patricia asked the teacher with a smirk on her face.

"What the book states," the teacher answered annoyed.

"1787," Patricia answered.

"See me after class Patricia," the teacher ordered her.

"Ooooohh." the class began to say because they thought that Patricia was in trouble.

"Silence!" the teacher ordered even more annoyed than before.

Patricia did not seem like she was concern or scared of seeing the teacher after class. Patricia smiles to herself. If anything, she should be scared to see me after class thought Patricia to herself. She had noticed that the teacher treats other black kids differently and unfairly compared to their white counterparts. Patricia settles into her desk in a very relaxed manner while anticipating a chance to talk to the teacher after class.

Finally, the bell rings. Most of the students look at Patricia before leaving the class. The black students seem concerned for her. Patricia had heard about how she talked to and treated the black kids when she had them alone with no witnesses present.

"Close the door after you, Johnny," the teacher said to the last student exiting the class.

He didn't reply. He did as he was told, and silently closed the door.

"Patricia, Patricia, Patricia," the teacher said her name over and over and over again in a mocking manner as she walks from behind her desk over to where Patricia is sitting. "What is wrong with you little monkey?" she started to taunt her with racial slurs by calling her a monkey. "You don't get enough attention at home? Is that why you want to stand out in my class and challenge the lecture or book information in my class? Okay, you have my attention, which I am sure you will realize very fast that you don't want it," the teacher said to Patricia in a taunting manner.

Patricia did not respond. She sat looking up at the teacher.

"Answer me you little shit!" the teacher said in an angry voice.

Patricia continues to look at the teacher, and a sinister grin comes across her face after hearing the teacher's insults.

"What are you smiling for?" the teacher asked annoyed.

Patricia decides it's time to put things into perspective for the teacher. Give her a reality check. When she answers, it was not in a little girl's voice. It was in her demon voice.

"Mrs. Reed, Mrs. Reed, Mrs. Reed," Patricia said in her thick, raspy demon voice.

The teacher becomes instantly frightened.

"Stay," Patricia said in her deep voice to prohibit the teacher from running. "Silence," Patricia ordered to prohibit the teacher from yelling out.

The teacher could not move or speak. She is terrified at the sight of the little girl moving her mouth, and a deep manly voice is coming out instead of a little girl's voice.

"I've heard about you and how you treat the black kids in your class. You have my attention Mrs. Reed, and I assure you that you will realize very fast that you don't want it." Patricia informed the terrified shaking teacher. "You have only treated the white students with respect. You played favorites. You have bullied all the other kids and even failed some who were very smart because you thought they were too smart for their own good due to their color. I must say those are piss poor teacher qualities. What should I do with you?" Patricia asked not expecting an answer.

The teacher could not answer. With the wave of her hand, Patricia made a chair slide across the room up behind the teacher.

"Sit," she commanded.

The teacher sits in the chair as commanded while still trembling with fear. Patricia looks at the teacher in silence for a while without an expression on her face. Her unnatural yellowish green eyes are staring intently at the racially prejudice scared out of her wits teacher.

"For so long you have bullied students of other races behind closed doors in secret," Patricia spoke slowly in her deep manly hoarse voice. "Many children cried themselves to sleep as a result of your words, your looks and your lack of compassion for them. Will you cry yourself to sleep tonight Mrs. Reed?" Patricia asked in a semi taunting way. "The human in you would tell you to tell someone about me. Also, to quit your job. You would do neither. You will keep me a secret or I will visit you not only in the classroom but in your home, in your bedroom, in your bathroom, in your car and definitely in the dark. My point is there is nowhere you can hide from me. There is no safe place for you. You are mine until I say otherwise. If you do as you're told, I will leave you alone for the most part. If not, your life as you know it will change into a living hell. I would even be in your dreams or should I say in your nightmares." Patricia said the last part of her statement with a deep throaty manly laugh afterward.

Tears rolled down the shaking teacher's face as she listened to Patricia and felt her laugh vibrate in her bones.

"No more bullying. Equal treatments for all students. Do not turn a blind eye when the white kids bully others. Do not grade students unfairly. Offer help to all the children academically who need it to pass in your class. Teach your children not to be racially inappropriate or prejudice against others as well. Be a better person, or I promise you I will punish you swiftly and harshly for every minute shortcoming or fuck up that you think would go unnoticed by me. A look, a gesture or a comment will be dealt with accordingly. Do I make myself clear Mrs. Reed?" Patricia asked.

"Speak." Patricia gave back the teacher her ability to talk again.

"Respond you wretched hag!" Patricia demanded raising her voice a little in a way that made the air go dense in the room.

Patricia's powers were almost as powerful as her mother's, Mistress. Patricia knows she could not let her temper get the best of her now. She would end up killing Mrs. Reed without even touching her. That is not her intentions. She intends to stop Mrs. Reed from being a bully plain and simple. She could not take on a pet at this time. The war is a priority. Pets take a back burner per her Mother's orders. Even the daughter of Mistress obeys her to the letter. No questions asked.

"Yes, yes, yes you are clear. I understand completely." Mrs. Reed finally responded due to being compelled to do so by fear.

"Good. You are released. I will see you here tomorrow and every day after. Don't call in unless you are truly sick or I will come in my invisible form and pay you a hellish visit." Patricia said with a sinister smile forming on her face.

The teacher's body relaxes and goes limp in the chair after Patricia releases her hold on her. Patricia stands up slowly. Her eyes turn brown to conceal the demon within her. She gathers her books and strolls over to the heavy breathing Mrs. Reed. She leans close to her right ear.

"Remember, treat everyone equally and tell no one about me, Mrs. Reed. I'll see you tomorrow. I'll bring an apple for the teacher." Patricia said with a broad smile forming on her face.

She quietly walks out of the room leaving Mrs. Reed in the room crying out loud like a three-year-old child. Funny how the bully reacted when someone stronger stands up to him or her thought Patricia as she closes the door quietly behind her.

To Claudia's surprise, Anya is in bed for once sleeping peacefully. Claudia enters the room in her invisible form. No door opening was needed. No sounds are made. She walks around the bed studying Anya while she sleeps. She leans in close to Anya's face. She can feel the breathe as Anya exhales. Claudia wants to make a dramatic entrance on Anya. So she leaves the room and flies out the window. She moves at the speed of light across the city until she finds the biggest tallest muscular man she could find.

She smiles to herself and says "Yes you will do."

She possesses the man's body. Using her mind, she teleports the man's body with her inside him back to Anya's room. Anya is still sleeping. She walks around the bed. Claudia gently pulls the sheet off of Anya. Anya stirs a little, but she does not wake up. As the sheet continues to come off of her, Anya instinctively wakes up scared and alert. Before she could make a sound, a large man's hand covers her mouth. Anya is scared out of her mind. She is paralyzed with fear. She sees the man reach for her sheet with his free hand. He puts a portion of the sheet in his mouth so he can tear off a piece of the sheet with one hand while keeping his other hand over Anya's mouth. He stuffs the torn off part of the sheet in Anya's mouth. Then he rips off a long strip of the sheet to tie around her mouth and head to hold the piece of sheet in her mouth in place. Even though Anya is making sounds, the sound is muffled by the sheet gag that is in her mouth. Now he is free to do whatever Claudia desires him to do. He pulls back Anya's head by the hand full of hair on the back of her head. He starts by slowly smelling the skin of her neck, then feeling her skin with his nose, his face, and his free hand. The man inside the host Claudia chose is getting excited as well. He is enjoying this very much. Claudia smiles to herself at the revelation of it all.

She says out loud to him "You haven't experienced nothing yet. We are going to fuck this little mean taunting spoiled whore into oblivion."

Anya almost passes out with fear after hearing the words that came out of the man's mouth. Claudia couldn't help but put the icing on the cake.

She says "It's me Anya. I brought you a special gift. A parting farewell special gift."

Anya knows who was talking to her. She knows it's the demon who has been haunting her, torturing her and turning her world and existence upside down. Also, she knows that tonight may be her last night alive because for the first time the demon used farewell in a sentence to her. The demon always told her in the past that it would leave her the day she dies.

"Good morning Terrance," Auroa said as she walked barefoot across the tiled kitchen floor.

"Good good morning," Terrance said startled. He didn't expect anyone to be up at 2 am in the morning. Maybe she couldn't sleep just like him.

"What are you doing up so early Auroa?" he asked.

"I always get up to get a snack in the middle of the night. It's a habit I am yet to break. Tonight I am craving chocolate ice cream. Care to join me?" she asked.

"Why not, yes I'll have a small bowl too," Terrance said with a smile forming on his face. Terrance watches intently as Auroa takes the ice cream out of the freezer. When she reaches up to the cabinets to get two bowls, her pajama top raises a little bit revealing nice full hips of curves and the bare skin of her stomach and belly button. Terrance feels his body get warm as well as his heartbeat and breathing increase. It's a good thing he has a five o'clock shadow on his face, or she would notice him blushing. This reaction is rare for him. He doesn't usually blush. Why does she have this effect on me he asked himself silently in his mind. She carries on dishing up the ice cream in the bowls while oblivious to the fact that he is staring at her. She has his undivided attention. She puts the ice cream back into the freezer, washes off the ice cream scooper, and places it dripping wet on the drain rack. She walks almost silently over to Terrance and places a bowl of ice cream with a spoon in it in front of him. She says "Goodnight" as she turns and starts to walk back to her room.

"You're not going to eat it in here with me?" Terrance asked half surprised.

"No, I always eat my snack in bed, crumbs and all," she replied over her shoulder through laughter.

"Goodnight and thank you," Terrance says to her back.

"You're welcome," she replied without turning around or slowing her steps back to her room.

Terrance eats his first spoon of chocolate ice cream and thinks to himself sweet and good just like you Auroa. A soft smile forms on his face as he eats another spoonful. Goodnight my fearless leader he says to himself while relishing the creamy texture of the high priced ice cream.

"Stay with me sweetness," Claudia said to Anya in the big man's voice she is possessing. Anya almost passes out from fear again. Claudia gives Anya a moment to stabilize her mind to keep her conscious. Claudia wants her to feel all the pain, fear, agony and hopelessness of the moment at hand as well as her ultimate soon-to-be end. The big man's hands slowly unbutton Anya's shirt and pants. He slowly undresses her. Claudia revels in delight as she senses that the man inside the body with her is getting excited. He loves every second of it. He loves the feel, the taste, the smell and the torture of Anya. She picked a winner this time she thought to herself.

"We are going to create a masterpiece, Donald," Claudia said out loud talking to the man inside the body with her. "A masterpiece," she repeated in a whisper as she exposed Anya's pink nipples of her large firm round breast.

The big man engulfs one of her breast in his mouth. Sucking hard while circling the nipple with his tongue. Anya cries out in pain as the man bites down hard on her breast to almost to the point of breaking the skin, but does not. His massive hand has the other nipple in an intense massage fondling frenzy. His mouth leaves one nipple to find the other. A moan of pleasure escapes him mixed with groans of pain from Anya. The sounds in the room are intoxicating to both Claudia and Donald. Claudia knows that Donald is a breast man. Probably stemmed from momma issues. Oh well, it will serve my purpose well thought Claudia. Also, he is an ass man. I will make it very entertaining for him thought Claudia as she made Donald bite down harder on Anya's right nipple. Anya arches her back in pain as her muffled cries fill Donald's ears. The big man's natural strength finish ripping the rest of Anya's clothes and panties off like they are toilet paper. Donald stops only to undress quickly. Skin against skin. All natural and uninhibited. Nothing is between the lamb and the wolf. Donald lowers himself back down on top of Anya. His weight is heavy to her at first. She could hardly breathe. Claudia takes note of it and adjusts Donald's body on top of Anya. She does not want Anya passing out from lack of oxygen or crushed to death prematurely. Claudia lets Donald take over at times. He is so caught up in the moment that he doesn't even realize that he is running the show for a moment. Donald lowers his mouth back down to Anya's breast while spreading her legs open with his legs. His massive cock is rock hard and ready to enter his prize of the night. Donald is in a state of ecstasy. He pushes his enormous cock inside of Anya. She is so tight. It takes a little force at first. He can feel her body being opened up wider and wider with every thrust deeper and deeper that he goes. Anya cries out in muffled pain with every stroke. Her pussy feels tight while becoming more and more wet with every thrust. She is so tight that when he pulls out, her body lifts off the bed some. Donald can't hold back any longer. He explodes deep inside of her as his cock's head hits the bottom of her pussy walls with one last great thrust. Both cry out, Anya in pain and Donald in pleasure.

However, there is no rest for the wicked. Donald pulls his still erected pulsating cock out of Anya. Even Donald is surprised that he is still hard. Claudia is taking his body to another level as she retakes control. The demon within is his own personal Viagra. Maybe sharing my body with her is not a bad thing Donald thought while already anticipating the next creative thing Claudia will do to Anya.

"Anya I have a treat for you. Do you remember what you and Billy did to Abby?" Claudia asked Anya.

Anya is instantly scared out of her wits. She remembers how cruel and hurtful she and Billy were to Abby. Anya remembers how she talked him into lowering Abby to the basement of the school where he violated Abby while she cheered him on and laughed at Abby's pain. She remembered how Abby begged them to stop while they laughed. Anya told Billy to do anal sex with Abby. Once her and Billy finished violating Abby, Anya turned off the lights and left Abby in the dark to find her clothes, get dressed and find her way out of the dark, deserted basement that haunted Abby's memories until she died.

"Now it's your turn. You will know how it feels to be hurt and be violated against your will like you had Billie do to Abby. Well almost like Abby. Abby trusted you and Billy. She was a true friend to you both. However, you and Billy found it amusing to target her venerability. You both found it amusing to betray her trust. You found it amusing to scar her for life. You found it amusing to taunt her about it every time you saw her in the hallways. You found it amusing to know that your threat of it happening again if she told anyone was effective even though you and Billy bragged about it to everyone all the time. It won't be at the level of cruelty that you and Billy did to Abby, but you will get the point while experiencing the act just the same." Claudia informs Anya as Donald turns her over and bring her up to her knees in front of him. While pushing her head and shoulders down on the bed with one hand, he guides his massive pre-cumming cock into her ass. With one quick movement, he thrusts his cock halfway into Anya's ass. Anya tries to make a sound. Her breathe is taken away by the pain. She feels like she is about to pass out, but without mercy, her body stays alert and take her agony over the edge with the pain.

"Stay with me sweetness. This is how Abby felt when Billy entered her, and you stood there laughing while getting turned on. Are you turned on now?" Claudia asked her as Donald gets deeper and deeper inside her with every stroke.

Now balls deep inside of Anya's ass, Donald is ready to explode again. He did not think it could get any better or tighter than her pussy. This is fucking awesome Donald thought just before cumming so hard that he swears he lost his eyesight as a result.

"Fucking awesome!" escaped Donald's lips as he felt his cock still ejaculating inside of Anya's tight ass.

"Was it good for you Anya baby as it was good for Donald?" Claudia asked.

That was the same question she asked Abby when she leaned down close to her that day in the basement and whispered in her ear while laughing after Billy was finished with her. Abby could only answer with her cries and shame at the time.

"Abby ended up killing herself as a result of your cruelty. You felt nothing when hearing the news of her suicide. You cared nothing for your actions. You just moved on to your next target, your next victim. You are a cruel bully with no conscious. Don't worry baby girl. I'll be your Jimmy Cricket. I'm your conscious." Claudia said to her with conviction. "Stay, I will be back. We still have some quality cuddle time coming up before you die in less than forty-eight hours," she whispered in Anya's ear as she disappears.

Anya cannot move. Claudia's demon powers made sure she stayed in place. Anya's body pain is too much for her mind to deal with, she passes out. Finally, she gets the mercy she never gave Abby.

Michael looks over at one of the low ranking fighters, Tally, who has been sitting in the same place motionless for about a half an hour. The only thing that confirms life still exists in her motionless body staring off into nothing is a tear here or there rolling down her cheeks at random. There are no facial expressions. Not even her long red hair moves on this windless night that is lit up with bright football stadium lights. Her eyes and nose are red from crying while her mouth is slightly open to breathe in and out since her nose is probably stuffed up from crying. Michael watches closely while waiting for the moment to arise or a gesture from the young woman that would indicate that she wants or needs some company to help her through the feelings of loss. Her best friend was killed last night, not by a demon or by any catalyst dealing with this war. A drunk driver killed her. A senseless loss of life because someone was drinking too much and decided to drive home just because she can as well as did not want to listen to reason from her co-workers. The drunk driver was not hurt hardly at all in the collision. However, Reda, Tally's friend, was injured severely. She fought for her life for six hours before she succumbed to her injuries and passed away.

Michael walks over to Tally and sits down by her side. He puts his hand on top of Tally's hands that are crossed over each other in her lap. For a brief moment Tally acknowledges the touch by an audible inhale and goes silent again staring into the air. Michael does not speak. At this moment words have no meaning. However, just knowing that you are not alone as well as feeling the touch of another being when she feels so out of touch and confused will give Tally a beacon of hope that there will be light again in her darkness from the loss of not only her best friend but someone who was like a sister to her as well as a light in the world. When Reda died, not only was her light put out, her death dimmed Tally's light a little as well. Michael squeezes Tally's hand gently, and a tiny smile appears on one corner of her mouth. Yes, there is still a lot of light inside of you Michael thought as he sits in silence at Tally's side.

Claudia has to make a stop and retrieve someone before returning to Anya's bedroom. She left Donald where she found him. He served his purpose well. He will be thinking about tonight for a while with a permanent smile on his face. Claudia made a promise to Abby. She promised her that she would retrieve her from hell for a minute moment in time to confront Anya before she finally sends Anya on a one-way ticket to the afterlife. Abby is in a very dark place full of torment and despair because of the way her life was ended. It would take a mighty demon such as Claudia to pull her out. However, it would only be short-lived. Not even Claudia could keep Abby out of that dark chamber of hell too long. Claudia does not like going to that part of hell. Not only are the ones who killed themselves tortured in all kinds of ways, but they are made to relive the part of their lives that made them want to take their lives over and over again at random times. At first, it breaks them. Then it twists their minds and turns them into the worst kind of demons imaginable. They are turned into lieutenants and generals in Lucifer's army. They become perfect demented, twisted unmerciful demonic entities that all demons except for the General, Mistress and Lucifer fear. Even Gabe yields and takes a step back out of pure fear and respect.

Claudia visits to Abby have become less frequent lately since Mistress has demanded so much of her time. She used to visit Abby at least twice a month to give her updates on how it's going with Anya. She hears Abby calling out from the abyss. It has been a couple of months since her last visit. Today Abby is getting her skin peeled off her body. Claudia puts her hand on the torturer's shoulders. He stops immediately when a powerful demon such as Claudia visits him. She gets not only his undivided attention, but she gets what she wants as well.

"Make her whole," she orders him.

It is instantly done. There are no questions of why. It is done out of obedience and without hesitation.

"Come with me Abby," Claudia orders.

Abby gets off the racking table and follows Claudia. Claudia remembers that Abby is not as powerful as she is. Therefore she can't travel as fast as Claudia does on her own. Claudia slows down enough to take her hand. Claudia will propel her upward and out of the pit.

"We have to go see an old friend of yours," she informs Abby.

"Finally. Thank you." Abby replied.

Out of the darkness and into the light they travel along with all of Abby's fury of hell with them.

Anya is right where Claudia left her. The only sign of life is her chest rising up and down as she inhales and exhales. Anya's eyes open slowly. Her eyes grow wide with fear when she sees not only Claudia standing at her bedside but Abby standing at her bedside as well.

"Anya I brought Abby here to say something to you," Claudia informed her in a soft low voice. "Abby," Claudia said gesturing with her right hand for her to go ahead.

Abby looks down at Anya for a moment and finally says only three words, "I forgive you."

Claudia is taken back a step. She didn't expect that. After all the torment that Anya put Abby through and all the suffering she is enduring every day and night in the pit, she still has compassion. She still is human to Anya. Tears silently roll down Anya's right cheek. Without a word, Claudia takes Abby's hand and leads her back down to the pit. Neither says a word. Claudia turns and leaves her in the darkness once again, but this time she is leaving Abby for the last time.

Claudia returns to Anya. Her intentions for Anya has changed with those three words. Before she was going to take her life. However, now she will spare her life as well as her parents' lives. Abby forgave her. She was doing this for Abby. Now that Abby has forgiven Anya, Claudia decided to let her live with conditions of course.

"Anya this is your lucky day," Claudia said in a low, slow voice. "You have been forgiven. Therefore, I am going to allow you to live and torment you no more with conditions of course," she said to Anya while cautioning her that there will be conditions to the truce and cease fire on her.

"The conditions are that you would not bully anyone for the rest of your life. You are to go out of your way to protect others that are bullied and preyed upon as well. You will create a memorial for Abby and openly advocate against bullying. Anya these are my conditions. Do you accept them?' she asked.

Anya does not speak. She only nods her head to indicate that she agrees.

"Anya I am very old. I assure you I will outlive you and then some. If you go back on your word to me, I'll make this session of torture look like a Catholic mass service. The wrath I would bring down upon you for lying to me would be cata-fucking-clysmic. Do I make myself crystal clear?" she asked Anya in a harsh demonic voice.

By the time Claudia had finished asking her question, Anya is shaking uncontrollably with fear. She is unable to answer right away.

"Answer me you swine!" Claudia demanded in her legendary demonic voice.

"Yes, yes I understand." Anya managed to answer after Claudia's order compelled her to do so.

As soon as Claudia heard the words, she releases her hold on Anya. She not only vacates the house, but hopefully Anya's life forever as long as she keeps her word.

Tonight is going to be different. Tonight Mistress is going with the fighters to look for the relic in the desert. Usually, she would send out her troops to search, find and retrieve on this mission alone, but tonight she is going with them. Even though Gabe is more than happy to have Mistress come along because he loves being in her presence, a lot of the other demons are not so pleased about it. If things do not go her way, it could be fatal for any one of them. Gabe walks into Mistress's chamber and kneels down on one knee.

"Everyone is ready Mistress," he informed her.

"Good," she replied.

Mistress stands up and walks toward the door. All Gabe could think is damn she is hot. She is wearing a tight black and purple leather dress suit with high heels while she carries her leather whip curled up in her right hand.

"My Black Queen," he said to her as she passes him while bowing his head.

She smiles a little to show she is pleased with his worship. Mistress walks through the big maple door to a room where about thirty demons in their human hosts are waiting for her instructions. She looks around the room and senses the nervousness in the air.

"Relax," she says in a low calming tone of voice.

"You should not think of it as Mistress is going with us or we may not all come back," she said calmly while looking into every one of their eyes.

"You should think that Mistress is with us. Nothing can harm us or stop us tonight," she said reassuring them that success is at hand as well as they won't fail because she is with them. A calm comes over the demons. Their human host facial expressions change to a calmer look. All the tension wrinkles are gone.

Mistress has a way about her that could calm the demons around her with the way she carries herself or the tone of her voice. She is a very effective leader and Mistress across the entire spectrum of emotions as well as actions.

The three jets are waiting on the runway to take them to the Colorado desert in California along the Colorado River. There a relic is believed to be buried in the Laguna Mountain area that borders the desert. Tonight is an important night for Mistress. It would be the first night that she finds her first relic of five that she would need to obtain to help secure her success and dominion over this planet. Once she has five relics, there will be nothing or no one who would be able to kill her, which would benefit towards her success of reaching her goal of hell on Earth. No one would be able to stop me she thought to herself with a slight smirk on her face. The flight is made in silence. Gabe sits on the right side of Mistress, which is fitting since he is her right-hand demon and second in command. The jet seating is a little different in her private jet. Her seat is elevated about one foot above the rest of the seats. Gabe's seat is raised about a half foot while all other seats are at equal level. Even in flight, she is superior. The silence of the short trip is only broken by the pilot announcing that they will reach their destination in two minutes and will be landing shortly. Mistress looks at Gabe and smiles in delight. Gabe reciprocates a broad, handsome smile in return.

The plane ride is smooth as well as quick. The landing is perfect on the makeshift runway that the demons had prepared the day before Mistress's arrival. Something that would have taken humans weeks or months to do, the demons did in a matter of hours. Everyone waits for Mistress to stand first before standing to leave the plane. She exits the jet first with Gabe following behind her. Then all the other demons did rank and file exit from the aircraft from highest to least seniority. Once outside, everyone loads into desert terrain utility vehicles. They travel towards the Laguna Mountain area. Mistress's Intel had informed her that the relic is in an ancient city buried within the mountain. They better be right she thought as they come to a stop at an opening that had been created by the demons days before.

Remarkably Mistress walks with ease in her high heels over the rocky terrain. It is as comfortable as breathing to her. The cave has been dug at a thirty-degree angle into the mountain. It descends to about two thousand feet, about six and a half football fields. It is a perfect circle about fifteen feet in diameter. As they draw near to the area of where the city is located, markings of hieroglyphics can be seen on the cave walls where the hole opens out to a city within the rock. It is a breathtaking sight even for demons. The demons have cleared away all the stone that was compressed around and in the city, which allows Mistress to walk in the city as it was long ago. It is a vast city with multiple dwellings big and small. Lighted torches have been placed throughout the city to give light to the matrix of the old winding roads. Mistress leads the way through the silent, desolate streets of the ancient city.

They come upon a three-story high massive building made of stone with one large door as the opening and windows. There is no glass in the windows like it is in our modern buildings of today. Mistress feels the presence of the relic. A smile forms on her face. She is like a child in a candy store. She walks in a hurry up the six stone steps and into the building. There is no light in the building. Two of the demons light flares that enable Mistress to see her surroundings more easily. The relic to Mistress is like a beacon of a Maine lighthouse to ships approaching shore from out to sea. It guides her safely to where it is located as she navigates with great ease over the cracked stone floor in her high heels. Mistress enters a chamber in the back far end opening on the left side of the building. She walks to the back wall and puts her hand on it. The triumphant smile on her face is revealing beautiful, perfect white teeth that seem to glow in the dark.

Mistress pushes her hand through the stone wall with great ease like a hot knife cuts through butter. She removes big chunks of stone until she could reach inside a little square pocket within the wall. It is almost like a safe for ancient time kind of set up. She removes a box that is wrapped in a cloth that falls apart once it is touched due to the age of the fabric. The box has more hieroglyphics on it. This one Mistress knows.

It says "In good hands save world. In evil hands destroy world."

Mistress smiles at the primitive description of the relic's use. No, she does not want to destroy the world. She will evolve the world into something way more sinister. She turns to her servants with a big smile on her face and holds up her prize. They all cheer with great enthusiasm. Mistress locks eye contact with Gabe. They share a silent connected moment with each other. As she looks away and starts her long walk back to the surface she thinks to herself; it's on little bitches, it's on. A foreboding smile forms across her face as her teeth glow in the dark. She whispers one word, "Michael."

Michael instantly hears Mistress call his name. He also knows that she has found a relic as well. Auroa wanted to return to her apartment to pick up some items before returning to Terrance's mansion. Auroa comes out of the bathroom with her hair wet and the towel half draped around her body. How come she does not think to cover herself up around him completely? It's as if she is in the presence of a gay guy or another girl. Michael is the best friend she has ever had Auroa thought as she walks out the bathroom and sees him sitting there waiting patiently for her to finish what she is doing to get ready for the day. He is someone who she can just be herself around. She does not have to worry about what she looks like, how she is expressing herself if she is eating as well as what she is eating. Auroa feels safe and thinks that he doesn't think that way about her. She is far from right. Angels do feel emotions of want and love. They love their father and want to please him. They love each other as well. Why would humans think that they would be void of love and emotions? They cry. They feel pain, betrayal, loyalty, love, hate, and loss when one of them dies or a human who they are close to is lost to death or lost to the other side of evil.

Michael forces himself to look away as Auroa comes out of the bathroom talking at random about how the apartment is not worth the money she is paying for it. The hot water was used up by the middle of her shower. Even though Michael hears her and her half-naked body is a pleasant distraction, his primary focus of thought is on that Mistress has found her first relic of the five she needs to help her win the war.

"Mistress has found her first relic." Michael interrupts her. Auroa stops talking and drying her hair. She forgets to breathe for a moment. She starts to breathe again.

"What what do we do?" she asked Michael in an almost state of confusion.

He looks over at her and says "We find our other four relics before she does." Michael replied. "Auroa there is a battle that is coming in a few weeks. I need you to be more focused than ever. There are ten holy churches in powerful places. We need to secure at least six of the churches along with our six relics as well. They go hand in hand with a victory for us. If we get six relics and five churches or vice versa, we will be at a stalemate. Neither side will have the upper hand, and things will continue as they are. The demons will consume humankind. The world as you know it would change. Not as drastic as it would have if Mistress won the war, but the world would slowly turn into a place where humans will not be the dominant species or have free will anymore." he informed her.

Auroa walks over to her bed and sits down.

"Why didn't you tell me about this before?" she asked

"You were not ready to hear it," Michael replied.

Auroa knows he is right. She was not ready before. She is not so sure that she is ready now, but it's time, and it's ready for her. Michael walks over to the bed and sits down beside her.

"Auroa I know this is a lot to handle. I am sure that the pace that I am revealing things to you will enable you to do so. I am here always to guide you, teach you and be your sounding board for as long as it takes for us to accomplish our goals at hand to triumph over this evil that is trying to consume the world. If you remain steadfast and focus on the tasks at hand, I promise there will be a light at the end of the tunnel." he reassured her.

Auroa just sits in silence. She heard what Michael said to her, every word. She just had to be still for a moment and let it all sink in. She makes a mental note of herself. She realizes that she has learned to be still in the midst of chaos. Michael notices it as well. He is very proud of how much she has grown in such a short period.

Today Mistress was able to give Lucifer an excellent report. It did not matter though. Even though he was very pleased, he still beat her and raped her anally and vaginally over and over and over again. His endurance is legendary. He is insatiable in his sadistic appetite. His abuse today was for the celebration of her pleasing him. It did not feel like a celebration at times to Mistress. She thought she passed out a few times from the intense pain Lucifer inflicted on her. It takes a lot of pain and torture for a demon to pass out because a demon's tolerance is so high. It takes even a hundred times more pain to make Mistress pass out, but Lucifer accomplished it like it was nothing. He is the Master after all. He is the only one who can torture, abuse and use Mistress for his pleasure, which he does very well.

Mistress lays in bed while letting her body heal from Lucifer's attack. Usually, a demon heals very fast, but it takes longer after an attack of that magnitude by Lucifer. Her mind drifts back into the past of long ago before she was known as Mistress and before she was the maleficent sadistic dominant demon that she is today. She does not remember when she was human or what her life was like before she died. Her time with Lucifer has removed all traces of her existence before him. Mistress was the fourth human to occupy hell after Lucifer was cast out of heaven. The three before her were killed for some reason or another in the past over time. Two of them were not missed by Mistress while one of them, Mistress was very close with her. If Mistress ever had a being she called a friend after she entered the afterlife, it would have been Celine, the third human to occupy hell. Celine was there for Mistress through a lot of her past hellish moments with Lucifer as she was there for Celine as well.

In the beginning, Lucifer was full of hate and rage because of his exile from Heaven. He is still full of hate and rage, but it is different today. He took his anger out on the four of them at random. Only one of the first four he confided in and favored. That was Zachariah. Even though he was Lucifer's favorite, he got tortured too, but not as much or as brutally as the other three. At first, Mistress, who was called Lolita back then, was

Lucifer's least favorite one of all. Mistress does not remember the first few thousand years with Lucifer because of the brutality he had inflicted upon her. The first few thousand years she was still partially human. After the first few thousand years with Lucifer, she lost all her humanity while she slowly started to make it up through the ranks in Lucifer's back then new novice of an army. Hell was never in short supply of human souls to torture, twist and turn into evil demons. Not all souls were turned into demons because not all souls were or are demon material. However, the first four were demon material. They were very good at being sadistic and evil. After all, they were created by the Master himself, Lucifer. Lucifer did not create all the demons, but the ones who he did create, not only became legendary demons but demon masterpieces as well.

Mistress has not had many regrettable days in hell or as a demon. Even the torturous days by Lucifer have not been regrettable days. Only one day stands out as regrettable to Mistress. That was the day Celine died. It was a day that would take Mistress over ten thousand years to recover from. It was the day Lucifer ordered her to kill her best friend, and she did.

By that time in her past, Mistress and Celine were two of three demons still alive of the initial four demons to occupy hell. Mistress was a first lieutenant. Celine was the third in command while Zachariah was the second in command to Lucifer. Celine had fallen in lust, not love, with one of the low ranking demons in Lucifer's army. Even though Lucifer had no romantic interest in Celine, he did not want anyone else to have her, and he definitely did not want to see her happy and smiling about someone or something that he was not the reason why she was smiling. Basically, he was jealous. He ordered Celine to stop, but she did not. As a result, he killed the low ranking demon in front of her and everyone to make an example of to deter and ensure that no one else disobeys his orders in the future. The only reason he did not kill Celine was that she was a very powerful demon in his by then experienced legion upon legion demon army. Over the next few hundred years, Celine grew more bitter and sloppy in her leadership skills as well as carrying out orders. Towards the end, she was downright utterly defiant towards Lucifer. Other lower ranking demons started to notice. Even Mistress talked to her one time. Her reply was simple.

"I don't care anymore Lolita. I just don't give a damn anymore."

Mistress did not pursue the conversation any longer. She knew that it would have been pointless. When Celine got something in her head or was on a path, no one would have talked her out of it.

Lucifer ordered Mistress to kill Celine because she was undermining his and everyone around her authority every chance she got. It was true. She even undermined Mistress's authority in front of everyone without even thinking twice. Mistress felt betrayed and greatly disrespected as a result, but not enough to kill her for it. Lucifer was far less forgiving. He wanted her existence for it. Mistress was even surprised that he let her do it for a few hundred years. However, she was not surprised that Lucifer picked her to kill Celine. Lucifer chose Mistress to be cruel. He knew how Mistress felt about Celine. He did it to torture Mistress mentally and physically as well. It hurt her being physically before and after she had killed Celine. That is the only kill that Mistress ever regretted. Lucifer relished in Mistress's pain and mental torture.

On the day of Celine's death, Mistress found her sitting on top of one of the mountains in Asia.

"I know what you are here for Lolita," Celine said in a low voice before Mistress had a chance to say something.

"Don't speak Lolita. I am ready. I want you to do it. I want it to be you. I won't fight you or resist you. Don't speak. Make it quick." said Celine as she turned her back to Mistress.

With one fatal blow, Mistress killed her best friend for Lucifer. She had done a lot of things for Lucifer, but this one would haunt her for many millenniums to come. Mistress went into exile to grieve for a couple of hundred years. Lucifer did not summon her. He let her be. When she was ready, she returned and rejoined the flanks of Lucifer's army. No questions were asked, and no reasons were given. None were needed. Both Lucifer and Mistress understood what had happened all too well.

Father Hannigan hates driving in the rain. He has to see the Archbishop, who outranks him. Therefore, he got the short end of the stick today, which is driving in the rain. The church was thinking about committing him to an asylum when he first tried to tell them that an angel, Michael, had appeared to him. He told the heads of the church that Michael said there is going to be many great and small battles against evil and that he would be a first lieutenant amongst the fighters. He was ridiculed as well as threatened to lose his appointed post with the holy church. That kind of treatment by the church went on for months until the day came that he was to be removed from his position and committed to a mental institution.

Father Hannigan remembers every detail of the day. He had just finished eating his breakfast that one of the nuns had brought to him. He was about to kneel down and pray in his room but was interrupted by a knock on his door.

The mild-mannered nun said, "Father, the Archbishop is here to see you."

"I didn't expect a visit from him today." Father Hannigan replied confused.

"He is not alone," she informed him. "I don't know the others who are with him. I have never seen them before," she spoke in a soft, timid voice.

The look on her face was confusion as well. Visits like this are never a good thing.

"I'll be out in a minute child." Father Hannigan informed her.

She quietly closed the door and walked down the hallway. Father Hannigan regained his composure. He knew in his mind what this was about. He had been warned to recant his statements about the angel's visit, or the consequences would be great. He had not done so. Therefore, he left them no choice, but to act.

Father Hannigan took a deep breath before leaving his room to walk down the long corridor to the staircase. As he descended the stairs, the question in his mind was what he would do when they lock him up in a ten by ten padded cell in a straight jacket. All he ever wanted to do was to serve the Lord. He would be lost if he could not worship and serve the Lord freely. He slowed his pace a little as he reached the bottom of the stairs. He could see the Archbishop and three other men he did not recognize waiting in the office for him. Two men were dressed in all white male nurse uniforms. The other man he didn't know was in an expensive three-piece suit. He is a lawyer thought Father Hannigan. I guess they are covering all the possible loose ends and liability issues as well.

"Good morning Archbishop. I didn't expect you here this morning." Father Hannigan said in a semi-surprised tone of voice.

He pauses for a moment to give the Archbishop time to introduce him to the other three men in the room.

"Father Hannigan this is John Thompson, a lawyer. This is Aaron and Phillip, they are nurses from the Terragon Facility in Williamsburg. This is Father Hannigan." the Archbishop introduced them all.

Father Hannigan took a moment to steady himself physically and emotionally.

"Archbishop." Father Hannigan managed to say when he was finally able to speak. "They are from the mental institution in Williamsburg?" he asked.

"You have given us no choice Father Hannigan." the Archbishop replied in a soft, sympathetic voice. "Father, I." the lawyer started to speak, but the Archbishop put up his hand for him to be silent.

"Please go quietly with the nurses. Let's not make this any harder than it has to be." he pleaded in a soft voice to Father Hannigan.

"I have never lied about anything. Why can't you believe in the miracle and accept it as truth? Have I ever misled or lied to you before? Have I ever given you a reason to doubt me? Please don't start now Thomas." he pleaded with the Archbishop.

The Archbishop turned his gaze from Father Hannigan and motioned for the two male nurses to take him. Father Hannigan did not put up a fight. He did not say another word in his defense. He let the two male nurses take his arms one on each side. As they started to walk out the room, Michael appeared in the middle of the room blocking their access to the doorway. The looks on the four men faces were priceless Father Hannigan thought to himself at the time. They could not believe their eyes of this tall beautiful, yet handsome man dressed in all white. He was much taller than all of the men in the room. The two male nurses let go of Father Hannigan and took a few steps backward. If they could have run out of the room without coming into contact with Michael, they would have. Neither one of them wanted to take that chance. The lawyer stood motionless with wide eyes and mouth opened. He did not even blink. It was as if he was scared he was going to miss something if he did.

The Archbishop fell to his knees and whispered "It's a miracle. Please forgive me for my doubt." he asked Michael.

"Father Hannigan spoke the truth. He has been chosen to fight in a war between good and evil. Do not persecute him any longer." Michael ordered them.

Just as quickly as he appeared, he disappeared the same way. The room was quiet for a couple of minutes. Only the sound of running feet broke the silence as the two male nurses ran as fast as they could out of the room. They both tried to squeeze through the doorway at the same time. It was comical to watch thought Father Hannigan. After a moment the Archbishop stood up and walked over to Father Hannigan. Without saying a word, he put his arms around him and started to weep.

"I am so sorry. Please forgive me," he said over and over again to Father Hannigan.

Father Hannigan returned the hug and said "All is forgiven, my brother. All is forgiven."

The lawyer stood motionless in the room still wide-eyed with his mouth opened. From that day on, the church has left him alone. He has even been offered a promotion, which he turned down because he would not be able to fulfill the duties of a new more demanding job because of his current obligations in the war. Anyway, Father Hannigan is perfectly content with his current position. He does not have ambitions to become a bishop or the

Pope. He just wants to continue to serve God and do God's will in the greatest war known to humankind thus far.

Edward stands up and walks over to her. Tonya is tied up on an inverted cross. Her arms are bound up and away from her body. Her legs are spread and bound to the ankle chains on the floor. She has a black leather ball gag in her mouth that is buckled around the base and top of her head. She only wears a black leather bra with silver stars lining the cleavage area. All her skin is exposed so she can feel every sting of his true relentless dominant power over her. He treats her like the slutty whore of a slave she is. She loves every minute of it. She is a real submissive masochist through and through. She lives only to serve him. Only Mistress has more power over her than him. After all, he is a slave to Mistress as well. She watches in silence as Edward walks towards her. She has been in the same position for six hours. He has beaten her at random multiple times for just existing. The dry blood covers areas where opened wounds used to be on her body. She, as a demon, healed her body with ease at first. Then as the beatings intensified and became more brutal, the healing slowed and the body she is in weaken. Following the last beating, it took her over thirty minutes to heal. Edward is not only a sadist, but he is also pure evil. He is third in command under Mistress and Gabe.

Edward touches Tonya's face. She yearns for his touch. All is pleasure; even the pain is a pleasure. Edward smiles as she leans her head into his touch. He lets her close her eyes, which indicates that she loves it. He slaps her as hard as he could across the face with his other hand. Blood flies across the room. A tear rolls down her right cheek. Edward's smile grows with his pleasure inside of him. He feels himself become aroused through seeing her in pain. He leans in slowly and kisses her bloody lips. She closes her eyes and yields to his touch. All she ever wants is for him to be pleased and his touch. It doesn't matter if it is soft or hard, tender or hurtful as long as he touches her and is pleased in all that she does as well as is enduring. Edward reaches up slowly and unbuckles Tonya's wrist restraints. He does the same for her ankles. She falls to the floor. The human body is weak. Edward grabs Tonya by the hair and drags her across the room to a table. He bends her forcefully over the table. Her breathing is heavy.

"Stay," he ordered her.

He walks over to his seven foot tall wooden upright chest. He opens one of the beautiful hand carved mahogany doors. The door is very heavy with large iron latches that require a key, which Edward keeps with him at all times around his neck. He reaches up and removes a leather whip from the top hook on the inside of the door. He hasn't used this one for a long time he thought to himself. As he walks back over to the table, he whips at the air making a loud popping whip sound. Tonya jumps at the sound. She knows what is coming soon. Edward feels himself getting aroused at the sight of Tonya's half-naked body bending over the table all exposed.

As he draws near, he reaches out and touches her softly at first. He enjoys feeling the lovely warm silkiness of her skin beneath his fingertips. He leans down and kisses the back of her neck, her shoulders, and mid back. Kissing, licking and nibbling as he goes further and further downward. Tonya moans in pleasure. He starts to caress, suck and nibble a little harder. He loves the way her skin feels and taste. Tonya arches her back. She is completely wet and ready for him. He makes his way down to her butt cheeks.. He pulls them apart and buries his face and tongue deep inside licking her ass and pussy with unrealistic nonhuman speed. Tonya does not dare say a word until she is given permission to do so. She just moans out loud in pleasure. Edward continues to drink every drop she has to offer while moaning in pleasure from her taste, feel and smell. He stands up and takes his massive cock out of his pants. Using one of his feet, he spreads her feet wide apart. While holding her firmly down with one hand on the table, he guides his swollen cock to her ass. With one swift movement, he pushes his massive cock deep into her ass. She yells out in pain, but he does not stop. As he finds his rhythm, Tonya starts to feel great pleasure from the fullness of his cock going in and out of her. Edward is lost in the tightness and warmth of her ass. It intoxicates him. He firmly holds one of her hips and leans in while he pulls her head backward by her hair. Harder and harder he rides her ass.

"You fucking dirty little whore," he whispers through tightly clenched teeth.

As he shoves his cock deeper and deeper inside her, Tonya's eyes roll back in her head and close with pleasure beyond comprehension. She lives for moments like this. Moments of great pain and pleasure. He rides her like the whore she is. As he is about to cum, he grabs her neck from behind to choke her until they both explode. Tonya loves it when he chokes and fucks her any way he wants to at the same time. It takes her over the edge and beyond. He chokes her just for her because she loves it. The only time Tonya is allowed to speak without permission is when she is cumming.

"Oh yessss, Hell yessss." she started to say before he began to choke the sound out of her. They explode one after the other. Edward let out a loud demonic cry. He slowly releases his grip on Tonya. Both lay on the table for a moment breathing heavy. Edward slowly pulls his cock out of Tonya.

He leans down and whispers in her ear "I am very pleased with you. To show you how pleased I am, I am going to use my favorite whip on you until you pass out." he informed her. "Would you like that?" he asked her, which gave her permission to speak.

"Yes Master, I would love that," she replied in a soft loving voice.

He kisses her cheek softly, picks up his whip and draws blood with the first lashing. A broad smile flashes across his face as Tonya yells out in pain. So nice to be Master he thought to himself as he brought down the second lashing on her bare skin. So nice indeed.

Mistress strolls through the halls of the massive castle-like building. The high ceilings and massive rooms produce an echo of her heels as she walks at a pace of going nowhere fast. Her thoughts are wandering from subject to subject at speed a human would not be able to keep up with. Her primary focus is on how to obtain the remaining relics that she needs to get that would give her an upper hand in this ever so lingering war at hand. She misses the old days when she was just allowed to exist, dominate and cause havoc at will that was laced with lots of pain and suffering of others. She misses the days that had no pressing matters to attend to. She misses where she did not have Lucifer making sometimes unrealistic demands of her. Realistically he is a strict Master to please. Very seldom does she reach his goals and expectations. The punishments are always swift and severe for her shortcomings of not obtaining his very unrealistic goals. Mistress has become accustomed to expecting punishment every time he comes to see her, which was not often before. He would usually leave her alone for the most part. He used to have other matters to deal with. However, this war has become his primary focus. He visits more often, three or four times a week. His timeline is off as well with his high expectations. He is not patient in any shape or form. He does not have to be. After all, he is the Master, and we are the Slaves. It's our sole purpose to please him, to serve him, to worship him and to be obedient to him Mistress thought to herself as she continues to stroll through the open corridor.

Four more relics need to be obtained as well as five holy places thought Mistress as she opens the heavy fifteen-foot high wooden door to another section of the massive building with ease. As she walks into another gym size room where about thirty demons are in the room, they all grow quiet. They did not expect to see Mistress come through the massive door.

"Carry on," she said softly to them as she continues her slow pace into the room. Even though the chatter and activity did not go on as before Mistress walked into the room, the demons did try to pretend to do so as she told them to do and carry on with minimal activity. As Mistress crosses the room, Edward catches her eye. She redirects her walk to intercept him as he walks towards one of the leather couches in the room.

"Hello Edward," she said to him in a soft authoritative voice.

Edward is startled. He did not see Mistress come into the room.

"Hello Mistress," he replied in a low submissive voice.

"What is the status of the project in Washington.?" she asked.

"We are still digging Mistress. So far we have not found the relic in five of the ten places your source said it might be located," he informed her.

He stands beside the couch waiting for Mistress's response. He does not dare sit down in her presence especially since she is standing.

"Edward, why do I need to find this out by chance?" she asked a little annoyed. "Why haven't I been kept more abreast of the situation?" she asked.

Her voice started to get a little louder. She takes a note of it and conscientiously calms herself.

"Mistress I am so sorry I.." he started to say, but she cuts him off.

"I don't want you to be sorry. I want you to be informative." she scolded him. "We should never have this conversation again. If we do, the outcome will go completely different than it's going now. Do you understand?" she asked in a soft low, authoritative voice.

"Yes, yes Ma'am. I am so sorry Mistress. It won't happen again." he responded in an apologetic submissive nervous voice.

"Now walk with me and tell me in detail what's been going on. After you finish, I want you to personally go to Washington and stay there until the dig sites are fully explored. You are to call me at noon and 6 pm my time every day with updates on your findings or lack of findings. Also, leave your slave here. I do not want you distracted. I want your head in my game, not on her. Are we clear." Mistress said in a firm voice, which indicated she was not only annoyed with Edward but impatient with his progress as well.

"Yes Mistress, very clear," Edward responded as they started to walk together.

Edward continues to brief Mistress of the past five digs as they walk across the room to the next massive wooden door. Once the door closes behind them, and they are alone on the other side of the door, Mistress close fisted backhands Edward across the face sending him twenty feet through the air across the room landing on a table. As Edward lays half on and half off the table trying to regain his bearing, Mistress walks quietly towards him at a slow pace.

"Edward," she began in a low, authoritative voice. "Don't ever make me have to come to you about anything of this magnitude of importance again," she ordered him as she leans down and talks close to his face. "You always come to me and keep me informed." she continued in a low voice. "The only reason I did not drop you to your knees in the other room was because it would have undermined my third in command with all my other slaves." she continued. "However, don't get it twisted. Next time I won't only drop you to your knees in front of everyone," she continued as she got so close to him that her lips almost touch his heavy mouth breathing lips, "I will kill you as well." she continued.

"Yes, yes, Mistress. I am so sorry. It won't happen again. Please forgive me." Edward said very nervously. "It won't happen again," he said again.

"It better not. Now pick yourself up, brush yourself off and give me the proper briefing I should have had in the first place," she ordered him as she stepped away from him to allow him to regain his composure and get up off the table.

"Yes Mistress, as you wish," Edward replied once he was able to stand upright.

"Good. Now inform me," she ordered as she turned to walk slowly and gracefully towards another set of double hand-carved wooden doors.

Edward follows sheepishly after Mistress staying a couple of paces behind her. It is no doubt in her mind, as well as in his mind that Edward will not make that mistake again. Mistress smirks a sadistic smile as she orders him "Talk."

Sleep had been somewhat elusive to her. Daisy is still mad as hell at Terrance for leaving her. However, tonight sleep could not hold her at bay any longer. Her body seizes it, and she falls into a deep coma-like sleep probably from sheer exhaustion. Usually, she does not dream, but tonight she is having a very vivid dream or is it a nightmare. In her dream, she is sitting next to a man on her bed, but there is something odd about him. His eyes are fire engine red, and his teeth are pointed and serrated like a shark. His voice is like music. She thinks he is a man because he looks like a man, but his voice is neither male or female at first. Then as time goes on his voice changes to a low, hoarse voice. A scary voice, but for some reason, she is not scared. Maybe she is not frightened because she knows it is a dream she thinks to herself.

"Daisy I am sorry that Terrance hurt you." the serrated, pointed teeth man said in almost a whisper at first. Then his voice got more audible towards the end of his statement. His voice sounded like he had a cold, a nasty cold coupled with a smoker's voice of someone who had smoked for many years. The musical voice had transformed into something hideous and sinister.

"Who are you? How do you know my name?" Daisy asked in bewilderment.

"My name is Azasar. I know a lot of things Daisy. I know that Terrance hurt you and abandon you. I know he broke his promises to you that he will always be there, that he will always take care of you and most importantly that he will always love you." Azasar said to her.

"Dreams, I just want to sleep in peace. I don't want to talk about what Terrance did or didn't do. It's over. I just want to sleep and move on." she replied as she started to crawl back into bed in her dream.

Azasar reaches out with his long fingernailed hand and grasps her shoulder to prevent her from lying down. "I have a proposition for you. What if I tell you that you can not only get him back but when he does come back to you, he would love you even more. He will marry you and your riches would be beyond your imagination. You would not only control him but his fortune as well. Do I have your attention?" Azasar asked at the end of his sale pitch. He knows he was deceiving her. He knows he is trying to trick her into helping him and his cause, but she does not know it. Her vanity and greed made her oblivious to what was truly going on. She does not realize an evil demon is tricking her. Humans are so naive and gullible, especially the greedy, selfish ones thought Azasar.

"You can't give that to me. This is just a dream. Daisy replied in a sleepy voice while trying to wiggle away from Azasar to go to bed.

He holds her shoulder firmly as he says "I can give that to you Daisy and much more. Much more."

"Okay, okay. Just give me sleep for now," she said while trying to bargain for much-needed rest.

"When you wake up, look on your nightstand. I will leave a purple rose for you, so you know I am real. If you want to talk to me, all you have to do is say my name, Azasar. What is my name Daisy?" he asked her.

"Azasar, Azasar, now let me sleep." she demanded.

Azasar releases his grip on her shoulder, and she lays down in bed. She falls dreamless asleep in her dream. Humans Azasar thinks to himself as he leaves her mind and her dream.

Jacob now understands why Trenton McNeil is a multibillionaire. The number of meetings, asset juggling, the bottom line in black or red monitoring and cutthroat receiving and giving business tactics alone should be paying him a billion dollars per hour. Jacob has taken over everything efficiently and smoothly. After all, he knows everything that McNeil knows now and more. He had turned heads and brought a lot of staff as well as competition into check with his swift I don't care what you think or feel kind of decisions lately, which is different from McNeil's touchy-feely emotionally involved at times decision-making habits. Jacob has increased McNeil's self-worth by fifteen percent since taking over his body with his decision making and business tactics. The stock has gone up, and the company is working more efficiently in the area of finance as well as personnel. This is mere child's play for Jacob. It is as easy as breathing.

"Sir you have a visitor." his male assistant's voice said over the intercom.

"Send them in," Jacob replied.

He didn't even bother asking who it was, which surprised the assistant. Mr. McNeil has been different lately, better, but different thought the assistant. The door opens, and Jacob gasps for a breath at the sight of the person who walks through the door. It is his sister demon, Alicia.

"Alicia, how did you find me?" he asked in a surprised yet excited to see her kind of voice.

"You are my brother. I always know where you are," she replied.

"Does Mistress know where I am?" he asked in an almost state of panic.

"Yes, but she can't touch you unless you are on the battlefield. You're fighting for the other side remember. Protocol prohibits her from going after or hurting as well as killing anyone on the other side of the battlefield once the war has started. So relax brother, you are safe." Alicia reassured him.

Jacob walks from behind the nice desk over to Alicia. Both of them embrace each other for a long emotional moment. Tears roll down both of their cheeks while they hold onto each other for a long time. Finally, they let go of each other, and both take a step back to put some distance between them that allows them both to look at each other's face.

"Jacob I am sorry about Telsa and Fione. I am so sorry brother." Alicia said while starting to cry again. Jacob reaches out and pulls her close to him to allow her to cry in his arms.

"Thank you, Alicia. Thank you," he says to her while holding her tightly.

Once Alicia crying seems to come to an end, he releases her once again.

"Jacob, what happened? Why does she want you dead as well?" Alicia asked. "Help me to understand why my brother is a traitor to his kind. Help me to understand why I may one day meet you on the battlefield fighting with my enemy." she pleaded with Jacob while staring at him intently with hurt and bewilderment in her eyes.

"Alicia." Jacob began. "What I did along with Telsa, I did for Fione. It was by chance that we came across Aztec with our daughter. He was taking her to Mistress. Fione was under a demon spell. Telsa and I didn't understand why he had our daughter. Why would he have her in a demon spell trance and above all, why he was taking her to Mistress of all demons. We asked him. Aztec being Aztec decided he was above us. He did not have to explain himself to anyone but Mistress. He always had that mentality. He was a mighty demon, so Telsa and I had to combine our powers to subdue him and bind him within his host until we found out what was going on as well as get him to take the curse off of Fione. Neither of us together or alone was powerful enough to lift the curse. Also, we did not know what curse incantations he used to curse her as well. It took us four and a half days of torturing to break him. Finally, he lifted the curse. Fione was scared out of her mind. Telsa and I asked her what was going on. Fione informed us that for the past eighty years she had been organizing other young demons to turn against Mistress while trying to find a way to end demon oppression under Mistress's control. Mistress had been suspicious that there was rebellion going on with younger demons, but she was unable to see it clearly due to a demon spell that hindered her from seeing what some younger demons were planning as well as doing. She put Aztec in charge of finding out what was going on with the younger demons and bringing the leader to her for punishment. Mistress wanted a public punishment of the leader to take place to deter any demons in the future from attempting anything remotely similar to what Fione was doing. We had to kill Aztec. We could not allow him to go free. We definitely could not allow him to take Fione to Mistress. Not even with the three of us combined, our powers were not strong enough to cast a demon memory spell on a demon as old as Aztec. We were left with no other option ." he explained.

He pauses for a moment and continues. "Aztec had found Fione and three other younger demons at a private meeting discussing strategies on how to recruit, implement resistance and carry out tactics of sabotage to Mistress's organization that would weaken Mistress hold on other demons in the long run. Fione and her followers were developing tactics that would give young and upcoming demons hope that they can be free to make their own choices, live not in fear from Mistress and above all be free of oppression, tyranny, persecution, and abolitionism of Mistress. Aztec stood in the shadows while Fione and the others had their meeting. He listened, and mind recorded all for Mistress to view at a later time once he presented Fione to her. After the meeting was over, Aztec stepped out of the shadows and revealed himself to the four young demons. Three of the young demons fought to the death trying to protect Fione and the knowledge of their cause. Fione only survived because Aztec was ordered to bring the leader of the resistance to Mistress alive. Fione was knocked out very quickly at the beginning of the fight. While the other young demons who were very skilled at fighting fought valiantly, they were no match for Aztec's strength and his fighting skills of perfection. He killed them off in seconds. Telsa and I were on patrol when we both felt that Fione was near. We were excited to see her since we had not seen her in about ten years. I know ten years to us is like ten minutes to a human, but she is our daughter. We were excited to see her just the same. We zoned in on her existence, and to our surprise, she was in a trance with Aztec. We questioned Aztec about what had happened to her.

He only replied, "Move aside, this is no concern of yours."

We informed him that Fione is our daughter. Instantly Aztec went into defense mode. He raised his demon sword and told us to step aside. He is taking Fione to Mistress. He would not say why. That is when Telsa and I locked hands to combine our powers. We sealed him in his host and subdued him until he took the demon spell off of Fione." He explained.

Jacob takes a deep breath and continues. "Then we had to make some decisions, some life-altering decisions. Telsa and I knew that once we killed Aztec, Mistress would know he is dead immediately. She would send someone out looking for his body and killer. Before we killed him, we sent Fione far away so she could not be linked or implemented in his death. We used his demon sword to kill him. We performed a spell that hindered Mistress from seeing what had happened with Fione and Aztec. We would have to tell her to reveal the details of what had happened, which was not going to happen. We waited with his body until Mistress soldiers came to retrieve him and us. It only took a few hours. We used the time embracing each other. We made love one last time. We talked, kissed, held and touched each other. Her soldiers found us sitting silently in the room with Aztec's host body holding each other. They took us into custody. There was no need to run and try to hide. They would have found us easily. Our demon essence would have led them straight to us. That is why we sent Fione away. They couldn't tell if Fione essence was present because she was there earlier or because we had been with her earlier. By staying and waiting for her soldiers, we protected Fione as well. Therefore, she was not implemented as being involved in the death of Aztec. Sister, for the love of my wife and daughter I am fighting on the other side against my kind. Family is everything to me. It always has been and always will be." Jacob said through tears that seem to have an endless flow from his eyes.

Alicia was crying as well. "As it is to me brother," Alicia said as she embraced her Jacob.

They held each other for a long time and cried freely and openly in each other's arms. Jacob's cause is now undoubtedly Alicia's cause as well. Alicia and Jacob together is a force that even Mistress would have to recognize and have cause for alarm. The office fills with sounds of cries that gave them both release while empowering their wrath and desire for revenge as well.

Azasar walks into his bedchambers where his two demon slaves are tied up in two corners of the room. Their hands are bound behind their backs and hog-tied to their feet. Both had a ball gag in their mouth. As he enters the room, both of his slaves look at him intently with the hope of being released for a while. Azasar had a long hard day. Mistress was even meaner today to him than she had ever been before. Her being mean didn't bother him so much. It's the consequences that could follow and be experienced by him as a result of her meanness that worry him. She could end up killing him with one of her mean streaks. Sonja and Terry start to mumble softly with the gags in their mouths to get Azasar's attention. He walks over to each of them. He unties them and takes the gags out of their mouths. Their mouths are bleeding in the corners and split due to having such a large gag in their mouth for an extended period, which instantly heals due to their demon powers. Azasar walks over to the oversized king size bed and throws himself on the plush burgundy feathered comforter and pillows. The two slaves walk gracefully over to the bed. One sits on each side of him on the bed. They did not speak. They know to wait until he addresses them or gives them permission to touch him. Azasar reaches up and touches each of his slaves with one hand which gives them permission to speak or touch him. His touch is like a power switch that has been turned on for Sonja and Terry. They both go into immediate actions of pleasing, touching, and caring for Azasar's every need and desire. They both were already naked. They slowly undress Azasar. First his shoes, one each. Then they take off his shirt together. Azasar lifts up his body and bends effortlessly in the direction he needs to help them accomplish removing his clothes. Then they take off his pants. Immediately after all his clothes are off, both slaves start to kissing and licking his body. Azasar buries a hand in the hair of each slave while holding their heads against his body. They both reposition themselves on the bed so they could both kiss him at the same time as well as kiss each other. The three of them did dances with their tongues in each other mouths while tasting each other through moans of pleasure.

Azasar's mind drifts back to Mistress. He instantly becomes aggressive and angry. The thought of Mistress always has that effect on him. He grabs a hand full of both of their hair, one handful of hair in each hand. They know that he is going to use them to take out his anger and frustration. It is times like this when he is upset and stressed that they both wish they had not chosen to be his slaves.

"Get on top and take it all," Azasar commanded Sonja. Azasar's cock is more massive than an average man, at least ten thick inches and even more at times. His girth is hard to take as well. Sonja obeys. As she lowers herself gently onto his cock, her facial grimaces express her pain. Azasar grows impatient and pulls her hard down on top of him. As he aggressively lifts and pulls Sonja up and down on top of him, he commands Terry to sit on his face. Terry is glad she got that command instead of the one Sonja did. However, she knows her turn would be soon to endure the pain that would have her sore for days. Azasar's stamina is legendary not only in the mansion but in hell itself. Oddly, both thought to themselves; this is going to be a long, painful night. Thanks, Mistress.

Tonight is a much needed night of relaxation for all the fighters who are exhausted not only physically, but mentally as well from training with the tireless angels. They never get tired Gregory thought as Gabriel walks briskly across the yard to the back door of the house. He has not seen his mother for almost six weeks. He has done nothing but train, eat, shower and sleep. He is determined to learn as much as he can as fast as he can. Terrance has been an excellent host to the fighters. He put them up in one of his mansions. He does not blink an eye when the training fighters are destroying his well-manicured grounds of the estate.

T'Ariel has learned so much these past weeks. Even though her focus is on learning fighting techniques and strategies as well as signals for battle, she has been focused on Gregory as well. He seems not to notice her at all. A couple of times she had small talk with him on purpose. He is very nice as well as intelligent. She hangs on his every word and laughter when they talk to each other. She feels herself falling for him, and he doesn't even realize that she is alive or seem to care. T'Ariel tried to get on Gregory's team of fighters, but she thinks that the angel in charge of making the final decision sensed that she was doing it for an emotional reason. Deep down inside she knows it is not a good idea because she will be distracted. She needs to be focused mainly during battle. Good thing an angel is looking out for not only her but Gregory as well she thought when her request didn't go through.

T'Ariel walks over to where Gregory is sitting and taking off his boots to put on his sneakers.

"Hey Greg what are you doing tonight?" she asked with a big smile on her face.

"I'm going home to see my mom. I haven't seen her for almost six weeks. I'm going to surprise her tonight. What about you?" he answered and asked without even looking up from his task of exchanging his shoes. He knew who it was by her voice. He is thinking about his mom. He is eager to get going as soon as he can.

"I may hang out with a few fighters tonight. I don't know yet," T'Ariel answered with a less of a smile on her face this time. The wind had been taken out of her sail when she heard that Gregory would be leaving the mansion tonight. She was hoping to spend some time with him. Gregory stands up and starts to gather his things. He is looking around for his other boot that had rolled slightly down the small hill. T'Ariel smiles, walks over, and picks the boot up.

"Is this what you're looking for." she laughs out loud a little.

He looks at her and flashes a broad smile. "Yes, thanks."

She melts inside as he reaches out and takes it for her hand.

"I'll see you in a couple of days," he told her as he turned to walk towards the house.

"Have fun," she says to his back.

"Thanks, you too," he replied without slowing his stride or turning around. She watches until he is out of sight. A couple of days without seeing you will be a lifetime she thought to herself as she starts to walk slowly towards the back door.

"A lifetime." she whispers out loud.

The realization of what Terrance did to her fills her mind as soon as Daisy wakes up. She looks at the clock on the nightstand. Daisy has been sleeping for over sixteen hours. She has never slept that long before. Her eyes widen, and she gasps. She stops breathing for a moment. A purple rose lays beside her alarm clock on the nightstand. Once she can start back breathing again, panic fills her body and mind. Someone has been in her home while she slept. She dreamt that she was talking to someone while sitting on the side of her bed. Maybe she was not dreaming, but it had to be a dream because of what the man looked like and how he sounded.

"Had to be a dream," she said the words out loud that she was thinking. Daisy reaches over and picks up the purple rose. She winces in pain and drops the rose back down on the nightstand after she pricks her finger on one of the thrones on the stem. That hurt. Yes, I am awake she thought as she puts her prinked finger her mouth to clean the blood off of it. Instantly she remembers what the man told her in the dream as she sucks on her bleeding finger. Fear and apprehension both fill her mind and body as she remembers that all she has to do is say his name and he will come. This is insane she thought to herself. It was just a dream. Well, a nightmare she corrected her thoughts in her head. Daisy gets out of bed and walks over to the bathroom. She opens up the medicine cabinet and takes out a Band-Aid. She slowly closes the mirror. She has to prove to herself that it was not real and that it was just a dream. She stares at her reflection in the mirror for a moment while getting up the nerve to say one word.

"Azasar." she said out loud looking at her reflection while not blinking.

"I thought you would never say my name. It's about time." Azasar said as he appeared out of thin air behind her. She is so frightened that she faints. Azasar catches her before she hits the floor. He picks her up and carries her to her bed.

"Humans," Azasar says out loud as he lays her on the plush mahogany sleigh bed.

The day has come to an end. The night is warm with a slight breeze. The kind of warm night that makes one want to take a nice walk on the beach. Even though the conversation came up to go to the beach for a while, May and her four friends decide to call it a night when May gets a phone call from a caller she does not recognize. At first, May ignores the phone call because she never answers phone calls that she does not know the number or know who the caller is. She lets her voicemail pick up the phone call. Once her phone notifies her that she has a voicemail, she listens to the call out of curiosity.

"I see you are standing there ignoring my phone call." the strange deep raspy voice informed her.

Fear, as well as a state of panic, fill May.

"Hey you guys, listen to this. Listen to this phone call I just received!" she yells out over her friends' conversations.

May plays the call for them. They all start to look around to see if anyone is close to them or watching them. They are near a bus stop waiting for the last bus of the night to pick them up. No one else is near or in the adjacent parking lots.

Tony and Roy put the three women between them to make them feel safe while they both keep a vigilant eye out for anyone who may try to approach them.

"Tony I am scared," Wanda says to Tony in a shaky voice.

"Me too," said Lee while biting her lips, which she always did when she was nervous.

"I am here. I won't let anything happen to you all." Tony said to make them feel safe.

"You stand here and " before Tony could finish his statement, he was lifted up in the air by something that could not be seen. Everyone started to scream as they watch Tony's body get twisted in midair and then pulled apart. Blood splashes on all of their faces as they stare in disbelief.

"Run, Run, Run dammit!" yells Roy to the women.

They start to run in the direction where there seems to be a lighted building in the distance. A loud deep throat laugh bellows out in the night. The demon is having fun tonight, but it is not just for his pleasure tonight. Edward targeted these five people for a reason. Two of the women are good friends with one of the first lieutenants in the human army. Edward cannot touch the lieutenants, but he can shake them up mentally to take their mind and attention off the battle coming up. Mistress gave strict orders that all is fair game, but under no circumstances are the demons to touch the human fighters or their families. They are allowed to how did she put it, "Mind fuck them through their friends at will." Mistress always has a plan that goes along with her master plan while staying within a set of boundaries that either her or Lucifer has set.

Tonight it is Edward's pleasure to carry out her orders in the most mind fucking manner he can muster. Roy leads the three women down the descending sidewalk towards the lighted building while yelling "Keep up and don't any of you dare fall!"

Edward laughs a loud demonic laugh at Roy's statement which seems to vibrate all of their bones deep inside. Even their teeth seem to vibrate while making a minute chomping motion inside their mouth uncontrollably. Lee starts to scream and run faster. She runs past Roy to lead the line of scared runners. Roy is amazed that someone her size can run so fast. She is pulling away from us he thought in disbelief. She is about ten feet ahead of everyone when it appears that she stops immediately. While her body is standing still, her head is twisted completely backward on her body with her eyes still wide open looking at her terrified friends. Wanda is too scared for sound to come out of her mouth. She mimics a person screaming without sound. She seems to be paralyzed and can't move. Roy grabs her by the shoulders and yanks her forward.

"Don't you stop! Run dammit Run!" he yelled out to the two terrified women.

They finally make it to the lighted building. It's an old stone Catholic church. Roy feels some sense of hope. Surely they would be safe in there. They run up the stone steps and burst their way through the tall double doors.

"Don't stop!" Roy yelled out as the women started to stop just inside the doorway of the church. "Run and find a place to hide!" he yelled out orders that he knew they needed to hear to keep them moving into the innermost part of the seem to be an empty church. For the first time, May falls.

"Don't you get all girly on me woman!" Roy screamed out as he pulls her to her feet and continues to run down the carpeted aisle of the large church.

The three of them run to the back of the church and go through a door that leads to a kitchen like room to the far right side of the church. They continue to open doors until they find a closet like room that is about eight feet by eight feet in size.

"Shhhh be quiet! Be quiet!" Roy whispered excitedly with authority. The women stop making crying noises. They all listen for any sound that the thing is still out there. The room is filled with heavy breathing.

"I think it is gone," May whispered as softly as she could while trying to stabilize her breathing.

The quietness of the room is almost deafening while the wait seems like a lifetime.

"I think we can go out now," Roy said after being in the room about ten minutes or more while reaching for the doorknob. Before his hand touches the doorknob a loud demonic laugh fills the closet.

"You thought you were safe. There is no safe place to hide.
There is no refuge, no escape, and no mercy!" Edward yelled out
in his demonic voice as he makes the room walls close slowly in
on his three victims. Mistress has used her powers to enable him
to chase his victims wherever they go even in a church. They try
to open the door, but the knob would not turn. Their yelling fills
the corridors of the church until they can yell no more. Blood
drains out the bottom of the closet door onto the kitchen floor to
be found by an early morning cook still in need of a morning cup
of coffee to fully wake him up for the day.

Daisy finally wakes up from her fainting spell. Azasar is sitting at
the foot of her bed looking at her in silence. He does not have
red eyes or sharp teeth like he did in her dream. He is quite
handsome with his goatee and dark blue eyes. Daisy always
loved dark blue eyes verse light blue. He has her attention, and
Azasar knows it.

"How is it possible that you were in my dreams and now you are
in my reality?" Daisy asked in a shaky voice. She is more
nervous than scared for some reason. She does not know why or
cannot explain it. Logic would tell her to run like hell, but for
some reason, she does not have the desire to do so. "Why am I
not running away and screaming like a mad woman?" she asked
herself not Azasar out loud.

"Greed," Azasar answered her even though he was not asked the question.

"How dare you come into my house and insult me!" she began, but Azasar holds up his hand and takes away her ability to speak. He does not have the time, desire or tolerance to hear her being a brat or for better words to describe her, a bitch.

While Daisy sits on the bed trying to make sound come out of her mouth, Azasar begins to speak. "Like I said I have a proposition for you. My Mistress does not know I am doing this. So if you fail, it won't backfire on me. We are going to test the water, you and I. We are going to see if Terrance still loves you. If he does, you will get close to him, very close to him. He will talk to you about things, and you will tell me everything. If I get the information I want, I will, in turn, give you what I promised to you in your dream. You will have Terrance back. He will marry you, and you will be in control of his billions as well as him. Later on today you will go to see Terrance and gain his trust. Work your magic to be back in his life and back in his bed. In turn, he will confide in you, and you will tell me everything. We both win. If you fail, I get your soul. That's the price for dealing with a demon and disappointing him or her." Azasar warned her while informing her of his intentions. "Do we have a deal?" he asked her while waving his hand to give her the ability to speak and answer him.

"Yes, yes, yes. We have a deal." Daisy finally said when she realized she could speak again.

Greed Azasar thought to himself. "It's not that easy, beautiful one. We must seal the deal." Azasar said with a smile forming on his face.

"How?" asked Daisy as Azasar came closer to her. He gently pushed her back on the bed while spreading her legs. This is a win-win situation for me thought Azasar. If she succeeds, I'll look good in Mistress' eyes. If she fails, I get her soul.

"I'm going to enjoy this," he said as he pushed his massive cock inside of her tight pussy. He didn't even wait for her to get wet. Their moans fill the room as his enormous cock goes deeper and deeper inside her with every stroke. His moans of pleasure and her groans of pain seal the deal that one of them will regret soon enough.

She woke up earlier than he did. She could hear the birds singing outside. The sunlight had just started to come over the horizon. She nestled her naked body up against his. Jordan loved the way Jack's naked body feels against hers. She feels his morning woodie and smiles to herself. She looks up at Jack's face to make sure he is still in LaLaland. The house is warm this morning. All they need is a sheet to be half draped over them to keep them comfortable. Jordan moves very slowly as she lifts up the sheet. Her smile broadens across her face when she sees Jack's thick hard cock standing at attention under the sheet to greet her. She lowers her body and head gently under the sheet. His body is so warm and firm. Jack stirs a little, which makes Jordan stop moving. She did not want him to wake up yet. Once she knows that Jack has fallen completely back to sleep again, she continues her decent under the sheet towards his rock hard erection. At first, she gently rubs her face against it, feeling the hardness and massiveness of it. Jordan feels herself instantly getting wet. She looks up at Jack one more time to make sure that he is still sleeping before she engulfs his cock deep into her wet mouth. The feel of his cock sliding in and out of her wet mouth slowly was intoxicating to her. She finds a slow rhythmic motion as a wet sucking sound fills the air. One hand massages his cock shaft while the other hand cups his cum filled balls. Jack starts to moan and wake up.

"Mmm Jordan." He manages to say as he turns over on his back to give her total access to his cock and balls. What a nice way to wake up with your lips on my cock he thought to himself. Once Jordan realizes Jack is awake, she increases her speed a little as well as suction, but not too fast and not too slow, just right as she deep throats his cock and swallows. She can taste the precum that escapes from the tip of his hard cock as Jack moans out loud in pleasure. His precum excites her even more. Jordan feels her pussy getting wetter. She wants him deep inside her. She has the urge to get on top of him and ride him until they both explode, but she resists. This morning is about him. She wants to please him this morning. She wants to worship his cock, her cock. If she could, she would tattoo her name on it. She gets more excited and increases her speed and suction a little more making sure to massage the head of his cock with her tongue while it is deep inside her hot wet mouth. Sloppy wet suction sounds fill the air of their bedroom. Jack reaches down and grabs a hand full of Jordan's hair on the back of her head.

"Yes, yes, just like that. Suck that cock. Oh shit baby, deeper, deeper." he says to Jordan as he pushes her head down on his cock. Jordan loves when he fucks her face. He feels himself about to cum. He pushes her head down faster and faster until he explodes balls deep inside Jordan's mouth. He fills her throat and mount full of cum. She does not let a drop spill out of her mouth. She sucks him dry and swallows it all. Jordan kisses the head of his cock and moves slowly up to his lips. She passionately kisses him and says "Good morning handsome."

"Good morning beautiful," Jack replied with a smile.

They lay in bed silently cuddling together listening to the birds singing. In a couple of hours, Jordan will have to get up to get dressed. She has to leave to prepare for the battle that is a couple of days away, which neither one wants to talk about this morning. They both just want to relax in each other's arms and live in the moment.

The day so far has been long and taxing on Daisy. For some reason, every minute has been longer and more tiring since Terrance closed the door in her face last night after rejecting her. She had never thought in a million years that he would do that. She feels a myriad of emotions from anger to hurt to even numbness at times. She never experienced rejection before especially for someone she let in her heart. Yes she knows she could be difficult at times and hard to live with as well as love and please, but she cares about Terrance in a way that she has never cared about another man before. She was and still is willing to marry him.

Thoughts in her head make tears well up in her eyes. Daisy fights back the tears as she crosses the intersection that has her upscale condo complex on the other side.

"Good afternoon Ma'am," said Ralph, the doorman.

"Good afternoon Ralph," replied Daisy.

Ralph is startled because she never speaks back yet alone call him by name. Being the kind concerned person he is, he had to ask, "Is everything okay Ma'am?"

"Yes, it is. Have a good day," answered Daisy in a soft voice as she gets onto the elevator and pushes the button.

Ralph had a glimpse of her face just before the doors closed. He could tell that everything's is not okay. He remembers that he has not seen Mr. Terrance around lately. He finally got tired of being treated like the help Ralph thought as he smiled slightly. He was not smiling because of Daisy's pain, but because Mr. Terrance, which he liked to be called instead of by his last name as his father, had finally grown some balls and stood up to her. The way she talked to him and treated him in front of people was a downright shame.

"Ralph can you get our bags out of the car please?" another tenant said to him interrupting his thoughts. Instantly he forgets all about Daisy and Terrance while he is busy performing the task at hand.

Daisy opens the front door of her condo and starts to cry instantly. She is not used to being alone all the time. She always needed someone to be with her even as a little girl. She had to be in the room with someone or something even if it is just a pet. She did not have any pets. She forbade Terrance to have any in the condo even though he begged her for a dog since he missed his dogs so much after leaving them with his ex-wife. It was always her way or no way, and he always gave in. He was always there no matter what. However, last night he showed her a side of him that no longer loved her, no longer tolerated her and no longer desired her. Her heart feels like it is going to come out of her chest. Daisy has never felt pain like this., She drops the bags on the floor at her side and lets her body fall to the floor while she cried out loud like a child.

Azasar has been watching her since she left the last store she was at shopping. He knows she is in pain emotionally and to tell the truth he does not care he thought as he watches one of the most selfish humans on the planet get what she deserves. She has not seen pain yet Azasar thought as he materializes himself behind her. He continues to stand over her for a while until her cries become a low audible whimper.

"Now now sweetheart, don't cry," he said in a low musical voice.

He startles Daisy. She jumps to her feet instantly and turns around to face him. She has her right hand on her chest while she breathes heavily. Her face is flushed with wide, scared eyes staring out it. Her fright is not just because Azasar surprised her. It is coupled with the flashback of their last encounter when Azasar sealed their deal. He was tender at first during their previous sexual encounter, but then he became brutal and savagely raped her vaginally and anally for what seemed like for hours. Daisy could barely walk afterward.

"What what are you doing here?" she asked in a shaky, scared voice.

"I've come to remind you that you belong to me now," Azasar said with a smile forming on his face.

"I'm not finished trying yet," Daisy said as she started to back away from Azasar to put some distance between them.

"Oh, sugar you are finished. That was a one-shot deal, which I may add you failed miserably at." Azasar informed her while taunting her at the same time.

"No, no, no he will come around. He is just still mad at me." Daisy tried to explain why he turned her away last night.

"No Daisy, I was there. I saw it. He doesn't love you anymore." Azasar said as he felt a surge of happiness in seeing her in such pain.

"Give me one more chance, and I can prove it to you that...." Daisy started to plea and bargain, but Azasar interrupted her and simply said "No."

"What does this mean now?" Daisy asked as tears welled up in her eyes and started silently streaming down her face.

"It means you are mine. You are mine to do with as I please when I please. I won't kill you now. However, from now on you may call me Master." Azasar said as he strolled towards Daisy to close the distance between them.

"No! No! No!" shouted Daisy as Azasar started to rip off her clothes while pushing her down to the floor.

"Yes! Yes! Yes!" Azasar said with a broad smile in response to her failed rejection of him.

"Now you will know what it means and feels like to belong to someone or should I say something that you don't control Daisy. You are mine, mine, all mine." Azasar whispered as he pushes his massive hard cock inside of her deeper and deeper with every stroke. He covered her mouth with his to muffle the cries of pain. He moans in pleasure as silent tears of pain roll down the side of Daisy's face. Yes one of them is regretting the deal they made, and it is definitely not me Azasar thought as he feels the head of his cock hit the bottom wall of his new piece of prime upscale juicy hot pussy.

Alicia sits in silence in the corner of the enormous center room of the west wing of the mansion. Her mind is full of thoughts of her brother, Jacob and the senseless loss of two of their family members, Telsa and Fione. The day after tomorrow she will meet Jacob on the battlefield. She along with Jacob have no intentions of fighting directly against each other. Mistress not only underestimated Jacob's loyalty to the family but if she thinks I will kill my brother for her, she apparently overestimated my devotion to her as well thought Alicia as she stares out into space.

She did not notice that Gabe had come up and sat across from her in the oversized leather recliner facing her. He has been watching her for a while before she realizes that she is being watched. She locks eyes with Gabe for a moment while waiting for him to either look away, leave or speak. He did neither. Alicia is not in the mood to entertain Gabe tonight. Therefore, she did not speak or look away as well. After a moment of stare and pointless silence, Gabe smiles slightly at her. Alicia did not return the smile or do anything that might indicate that she wanted his company tonight. Gabe has always had a fondness for Alicia even though she never gave him the time of day. Maybe he thought she was smart, funny or hell even beautiful, but Alicia never cared one way or another, and she was not about to start caring now.

"What are you thinking about Alicia?" Gabe asked with a smile while not taking his eyes off of her.

"Gabe not tonight. I am not in the mood for conversation tonight," she said with a sigh.

There has never been anything romantic between the two of them, but for some reason or another Gabe has always given her his undivided attention if she was in the room unless Mistress was in the same room of course. He is her boss, and he is a little too ruthless for her taste. He can be funny sometimes, but a sense of humor would only take him so far with Alicia. Gabe does not reply to her statement. Instead, he acts like she never said anything. He continues to sit there with that ridiculous smile on his face and stares at her. After a moment his smile fades. He stands up and walks briskly away without saying a word. His Mistress is summoning him. Good, Alicia thought as she let her thoughts drift back to her brother and the battle ahead.

Michael sits in Auroa's apartment at the kitchen table with Uriel and Gabriel. The three of them need to be on the same page regarding the events that are to transpire in the days ahead. Also, there is a great concern that the fighters, as well as Auroa, might not be ready. The battle will be in a few days, not months, but days. The three angels have been working around the clock training the fighters on different shifts to teach smaller groups to enhance the training and to give individualized attention to some soldiers that were needed. A lot of the weaknesses of the fighters have been corrected, but there are still a few problem areas that could cause significant casualties if left not corrected.

"Michael," Uriel began " some of the fighters are not ready for a battle of this magnitude," he informed Michael in his musical angelic voice.

"I know Uriel." Michael agreed. "but they have something else on their side. They have heart and an overwhelming desire to win. They fight with their heart and soul for God. They will prevail or die trying. I would take that any day over skills and someone who is not fighting with their heart and soul. It is our job to train them and work out all the kinks and shortcomings that we can. We already know that the first battle will have a larger number of casualties than the second, third, fourth and fifth battles. We know that their experiences, as well as their skills, will get better with each battle and time as well as training." Michael explained to Uriel and Gabriel. "Our job is to train them, guide them and direct them in the course of actions during the fight to minimize the causalities. There will be loss. We must prepare them for this as much as possible." Michael said in a low empathetic voice. "The battle will take place a hundred miles south of here in an area where the first church was built. There is no human population within a fifty miles radius. It is mostly overgrown with trees and wildlife. We will start transporting the fighters today. We will have at least four hundred fighters in place with at least twenty-first lieutenants and forty-second lieutenants. Auroa will have an earpiece that gives the lieutenants direct communication with her, myself and you two as well." he informed them.

"I have a surprise for you two to pass on to the angels that are in your charge. This fight against evil is different from the ones in the past. We are permitted to fight and direct in the battles. In the past, we were made to stand on the sidelines and watch the brave humans die mercilessly at the hand of powerful demons. Now we are leveling the playing field. This is a great advantage. The demons cannot kill us. They can only send us back to heaven where we will only regroup and return almost immediately even more powerful than before." Michael continued. "So go and organize your transport of the fighters. Tell the angels who you are in charge of to get ready for battle. Pray to God Almighty for a victory." he ordered Gabriel and Uriel.

"By the way, only fifty angels are allowed to go into each battle. We have to keep a balance and give the humans most of the fight. It is the will of God that they do most of the fighting against evil to protect the Earth, which he has given to them with their bodies, hearts, and souls." Michael instructed them. The last statement answered a question that Gabriel was about to ask. Why not let the angel go in and kill them all. Michael saw the questioning look on Gabriel 's face and answered the question before he had a chance to ask it. Michael stands up and looks towards Auroa's bedroom. He could sense that she is still sleeping. She wanted to sleep in her apartment last night for some reason. It is still early in the morning. She went to bed pretty late last night. He kept her up briefing her on tactics and strategies of warfare. She showed great promise. She did not complain or seem to tire. Michael had to tell her it was time for her to go to bed. After all, angels do not sleep. He could have gone on forever, but Auroa would not be worth anything if she does not get the sleep that she needs. Gabriel and Uriel stand up, and both of them nod farewell to Michael. They silently disappear to carry out Michael's orders. Michael sits back down at the table and waits patiently for Auroa to wake up.

"Sleep well my Captain," he said in a low whisper as Auroa continues to dream about her greatest fear, the death of the people she is leading into battle.

"Azasar, I want everything and everyone ready for transport by tomorrow morning. No excuses, no oversights, and no fuckups. Do I make myself clear?" Mistress asked in a low irritated tone of voice.

"Yes Mistress, very clear," Azasar answered her in a shaky submissive voice. Mistress has been upset with him ever since he blotched the abduction of the first lieutenant, Jordan and caused the death of several of her demon servants. The only reason Azasar is not dead is that he is very skilled at organizing and the strategies of battle. Mistress knows she has to think about the bigger picture. It is not about him or how she feels about him now. Lucifer would have her head over and over and over again after he killed her and revived her over and over again if she compromises the possibility of winning the war due to her personal feelings towards Azasar. However, that doesn't mean she has to be nice to him or like it. She controls herself from releasing her wrath on him. Although, a lowly ranking demon in the room might not be so lucky. Azasar, as well as the other demons, know what Mistress is doing. They try very hard not to be in the room with Mistress and Azasar at the same time. Mistress has killed six demons and injured ten others to the point it took days for them to recover because they were in the same room with Mistress and Azasar during a discussion. Azasar, who is the fourth in command is apparently living on borrowed time.

"Mistress I have intelligence that says that the humans are starting to deploy to the area as we speak," Azasar informed Mistress.

"Do you now?" she asked in a taunting voice before she could stop herself.

She takes a deep breath and makes a conscientious effort to be tolerable of Azasar in her presence, in her room, in her house, in the same state, in the same country, and on the same planet that she is on. All of this went through her head in a minute whisper in time before she spoke her next words to Azasar.

"Yes Azasar, they have started to deploy to the area. We do not need to go today. Even though we could get there and kill them all as they arrive, there are certain rules, protocols, and etiquettes that we must follow in a war such as this to make the right of passage of the relic or a holy land site to pass to the winner officially. Remember they are merely humans. They are nowhere near as powerful as we are. So rules, protocols, and proper etiquettes were put in place to level the playing field. If we go in before to wait and destroy the human fighters when they arrive, we would not be given the power count of the relic or the holy site that we would have obtained after a victory as a result of it. We have bigger problems Azasar. I have just found out that this war is a little different. One of the protocols to change is that up to fifty angels can fight with the humans in each battle. Demons do not have the power to kill angels, even though angels can kill demons. What the Fuck! How in the hell is that a level playing field?" Mistress asked between angry clenched teeth after explaining with great composure the Do's and Don'ts of battle with the humans.

Azasar stands in silence waiting for Mistress to calm down. He knows he should not say anything to her when she is upset, especially since he is already in the fire and not the frying pan. After a few minutes, Mistress calms down and looks reluctantly at Azasar. She is so irritated with him that she hates to even look at him. However, she is all about control. How can she control others if she can't even control herself?

"Azasar no fuck ups. Make sure everything is in place," she ordered in a low steady tone of voice.

She holds her gaze on him for a moment. Afterward, she turns and walks away gracefully out of the room. Azasar started to breathe again.

Patricia sits in silence in the deserted park. It is too chilly this evening for most children to be out this late. She is not thinking about anything in particular. She is letting her mind relax while she is enjoying her time to herself away from humans and demons alike. She always enjoys being alone. Unlike her Mother, she does not always have to be the center of attention or in the middle of a chaotic moment most of the time. That is one of the things her Father, Lucifer, loves about her the most. A small breeze fills the once still air and leaves swirl around her in no set pattern. Patricia begins to swing back and forth in the swing without her feet leaving the ground. How relaxing she thought to herself as she lets her eyes close for a moment.

All of a sudden she opens her eyes. She realizes that she is not alone. "Hello, Father," Patricia said in a low little girl's voice.

"Hello, Patricia," Lucifer says to her in a low tender voice as well. One could hear affection of endearment in his voice as he spoke to Patricia. For a moment both sit in silence just enjoying each other's company. Although Lucifer is not visible, Patricia knows he is there and sitting in the swing right beside her.

"Patricia," Lucifer said tenderly breaking the silence between them.

"Yes, Father?" Patricia responded.

"How do you feel about the war we are going to fight?" he asked while still maintaining a low tender voice.

"It is what it is Father and is necessary," she replied. "It is a step in evolution that has to take place for us to take our rightful place on Earth." she continued.

While she was talking, Lucifer materialized a little in a semi-transparent form. She looks up at him and a smile forms on his face. Patricia is his most favorite child, even more so than his firstborn son. She is more powerful now than all of his other children put together. In two years when she turns three hundred years old, her power will be second only to Lucifer. Not even Mistress will stand in her shadows. Another moment of silence passes between the two of them. They both enjoy each other's company. They relax and ground one another naturally. Mistress, as well as Lucifer's other children, have always been very jealous of their relationship. They are deadly jealous to be precise. Patricia is still alive because it is the will of Lucifer and all of them know that if they harm her, they will die a legendary death. That goes for Mistress and all his children. However, there is one who may test the water and take a chance if the moment arises, his firstborn son Xzavia. The thought of Xzavia harming Patricia makes Lucifer upset. Patricia senses his inner turmoil. "What troubles you Father?" she asked in a sweet little girl's innocent voice.

Lucifer makes a successful effort to calm down before he speaks. His voice is tender and affectionate as he answers Patricia. "Patricia you know that my son Xzavia has feelings for you. He has mixed feelings. On the one hand, he wants you as his bride one day, which I have forbidden. On the other hand, he is very jealous of you because of our bond with one another and how powerful you will become in two years on your three hundredth birthday." he answered. Before she could respond, he continues. "Xzavia is going to try to win your affection and hand in marriage soon."

"I have no desire to be his Father." she interrupted.

"I know my child, but he will try just the same. When you reject him, he will try to kill you against my wishes." Lucifer informs her. "I need you to be even more vigilant than before. I will protect you, but there will be times my attention will be elsewhere. If he succeeds in killing you, I assure you I will annulated his existence in a way that even I will be amazed." he assured her after giving her warnings and instructions concerning her half-brother.

"Father I have a question. What if I end up killing Xzavia in my defense?" she asked cautiously.

"As long as you are defending your existence, he dies, he dies," Lucifer answered her. "You are more important to me than he would ever be," he assured her.

No other words were spoken between the two of them while she and Lucifer remain in the park for a couple more hours together. They sit in silence and just enjoy the comforting and relaxing feelings of just being close to each other. After a couple of hours have passed, Lucifer slips away as silently as he had arrived.

The old white church is abandoned in the middle of nowhere. There is not a house or business within miles. A hundred years ago the church was the pillar of a small thriving town of about three hundred people. While little by little the kids grew up and moved away, older people in the town died, and the little town died along with them. The paint of the church is peeling under the overgrown vines. The tall one-story wooden church has stood the test of time. A few windows in the front are broken out as a result of drunken hunters who practiced their lousy shooting skills at a target that stood still unlike the moving live targets that they could not focus enough on in their drunken state to shoot. The only remnant of the town left is the old graveyard that sits off to the far right of the church on a steep hill. Some of the graves stones are cracked and stained due to weathering the elements of time, while others seem to stand the test of time. Some names could not be read while other names appear as though they were written yesterday. The well-preserved headstones stand out and look as though they were newly placed in the weather-beaten graveyard. The newer looking gravestones are well preserved because they are close to a row of a tall, weathered stone wall. It protected the headstones from the wind, the sand and the rain that broke down as well as aged the other headstones with time's harsh elements of erosions. For some unknown reason, the grass and weeds did not overtake the graveyard as it did the church and the rest of the surrounding area. It is like the grass only grows a certain height and stops around and near the graveyard. The green lush flowing grass is ankle high that flows in the direction of the wind that causes it to look like green waves of an ocean. The sight is memorizing. If one stares at it for a while, one can almost imagine hearing the waves of an ocean from the sound of the blowing wind and swaying grass. The beautiful waves of grass flow with the wind up to the first row of gravestones and then almost nothing. The grass around the headstones could not be any taller than a couple of inches. It is uncanny how low the grass is in the graveyard itself. The church and the cemetery are at the center of the holy ground area that needs to be won by either good or evil. They are surrounded by a forty mile radius of holy land. The main battle will take place ten miles north of the church in a clearing that is the size of four football fields. Some protocols have to be followed such as the battle can't begin until noon tomorrow. Also, the fighters will be on the opposite side of the field facing each other while Mistress and Auroa walk alone to the center of the field to introduce themselves to each other for the first time. They will greet each other the same way before all the future battles as well. Neither is allowed to hurt the other, or they will automatically forfeit winning at all in the overall war itself. Once the formalities are over between Mistress and Auroa, each will return to a safe position on their perspective sidelines. They will wait for the stroke of noon to begin the battle using knives, swords, axes, clubs or any other weapon of choice except for guns, bombs, mechanical weapons or chemical weapons. The fighting techniques will be that of the old age. Modern technology will not be used or manipulated to give one side an upper hand over the other. When humans first heard this, one of them asked how they are supposed to win.

Michael replied, "Through skill, endurance, desire to prevail and sheer determination to win for all of humanity of today and future generation to come." He continues, "You will fight as if your very existence hangs in the balance because it does. All the lives of your children, your mother, your father, your sister, your brother, your wife, your husband, and all the loved ones you hold so dear are on the line. Win they live, lose they die. Fight for life over death. That is how you win." Michael answered.

Over the past few months, the humans have given all they have to learn combat fighting techniques that are allowed in the battle zone to ensure a winning chance on the day of reckoning.

Michael, Auroa and the other angels are very pleased with the fighters commitment, endurance and determination to be the best they can be. The fighters learned all they could in the limited amount of time they had as well as under the conditions they had to learn. Some of them never had a fight in their lives. Some are very small and weak in strength, but all are big in courage, character, honor, and determination to give all they have in a fight until a win or until death, whichever one comes first. No one could ask anything greater than that of a worrier on the battlefield.

Each battle will only last for sixty-four minutes. Not only was the number sixty-four significant in the body sacrifices to start the war, but it is vital in determining the number of major battles as well as the minutes for each battle that the demons are allowed to fight with the humans. There will be five major battles. Therefore, there needed to be five separate sacrifices of sixty-four bodies as well, hence the five crime scenes. A body for every minute that the demons are allowed on the battlefield to fight the humans on Earth. At the end of the sixty-four minute, all the fighting will cease. Then it will be determined who won the battle. A bright almost blinding light will appear over the middle of the battlefield and then drift over to the side that won the battle. The decision is absolute and cannot be disputed by either party. Who determines which side wins is unknown. All is known is that the decision is final.

A fog is settling over the battlefield. It is not a full white out. The cloud seems to linger at the grass line only as if gravity would not let it rise above the knees. It is as if gravity understands the seriousness of the visibility that would be needed in the battle that is on the horizon. As the two opposing sides begin to settle on their side of the field, little talk or conversation is occurring. The silence speaks volume. The anticipation, the concentration, the apprehension, the uncertainty and the wait are apparent in the air, which almost makes the air heavy. It is as if one could use a knife to cut the invisible air into slices. For some, the realization of the moment and soon to be future moments have left them feeling like they are in a daze. Some even inflicted a little pain on themselves to give themselves a reality check to help them determine that this is not a dream. A little pain to let them know that they are still alive before dying. Kisses and hugs have been given to loved ones through possible goodbye tears on both sides, demons and humans alike. Both sides realized that they might be seeing their loved ones for the last time. Unlike humans, demons do not go to an afterlife when they die. Death for a demon means no more existence anywhere. No purgatory or hell for them. There is just nothing. It is as if they just evaporate into thin air as light rain does on a hot day off the hot pavement. They vanish into thin air to exist no more. There is fear on both sides of the battlefield. For tomorrow both sides will have loses. Only the angels have an advantage of returning to see a battle another day. The host body of the angel can be damaged so that it cannot use it anymore, such as cutting off a head and limbs. Other wounds could be healed almost immediately by the angels. The demons are very skittish about fighting the angels. The angels could kill them, but they cannot destroy the angels. The demons are prohibited from leaving their host body during battle. Therefore, that means that they can be killed in the host body as well. The angels do not have those restrictions because the angels are there to balance or level the odds in the battles. Even though fifty angels could fight in each battle at one time, the demons still have the advantage over humans with speed, strength, endurance, fighting skills, and healing abilities. Also, the demons can continue to fight hard even though the host body is gravely wounded. Humans are at a great disadvantage in all of those aspects when it comes to fighting on the battlefield tomorrow. The humans would have to rely on pure adrenaline, determination and the sheer will to fight until they cannot fight anymore, to win or die while trying.

Michael, Auroa, and Jordan sit in silence on the plane ride to the battleground. Each one of them is deep in their thoughts. Michael is thinking about the battle itself. The casualties will be high. He hopes that it will not deter some of the fighters to remain hopeful. Michael wants the soldiers to continue to fight while giving it all that they have to give to ensure a possible win. Without hope, all would be lost before it is even really starts.

Michael has always carried the burden of worrying about the humans and their wellbeing as a whole. While the other angels do care, they are a lot more detached from feeling for the humans as well as about them. A true leader has to care about the ones under him or her genuinely to lead them properly Michael has always believed. He wants what is best for them because his father made them. Even though God has asked him to love them, he loves them freely just because he simply does with his heart and being as well.

At first, Auroa is thinking about her parents who the angels have already made sure they are somewhere safe. Her parents were put in a place that not even Auroa knows where. The angels did it to put Auroa's mind at ease. They did not want Auroa to worry about her parents even though the demons cannot touch them because of the protocol. The fighters' families are off limits while friends are fair game. Also one of the protocols of battle is that demons cannot possess Auroa, the fighters, and their families. If the demons do violate protocols, they will forfeit their chance to win the War. However, the demons have other tactics that could be used to find out information. Just like when Azasar killed and possessed Jordan's friend to get to her. Friends are fair game indeed Auroa thought to herself as she stares off into space.

Auroa's thoughts shifts to her soon to be meeting with the demon Mistress who she has heard so many horrible things about. She will soon be standing face to face with pure evil. She hopes that she would not buckle in her presence. She hopes that she remains an inspiration to all the fighters who she is leading who are watching her walk out onto the center of the field. Not only is she proud of every one of them, but she also hopes that they are proud of her as well.

Jordan's mind is on her husband that she made love to earlier that morning one last time before leaving to go to her boys' rooms to kiss them goodbye and hold them in her arms one last time. Matthew asked her why she was crying.

"I am just so happy to be right here, right now holding you handsome," Jordan replied.

He squeezed his mother tighter and said, "Me too mommy."

Alex was still sleeping and did not want to wake up. He slept through her hugs and kisses of goodbyes. He snuggled into his pillows again after she released him. So peaceful and oblivious to what is going on Jordan thought to herself. For you, I will fight today. For all of you, I will fight to help us to claim victory over evil today Jordan said silently in her head while looking at them for a long moment.

"I love you all," Jordan whispered out loud as she closed the front door of the house to leave that morning.

On the plane, she motivates herself by thinking about what she will do when she gets back home. The thought of it makes a little smile form on her face. There is light in the midst of darkness she thought to herself as the plane starts to descend for landing.

Gabe has to be the most apparent pumped up demon on the field. His body is on high alert with his chest lifted and thrust forward as he walks at a fast pace from soldier station to soldier station inspecting gear, positions, and attitudes of the fighters. He is focused on only two things, winning and making Mistress proud as well as happy. When he speaks to the other demons, it is not with compassion or empathy. It is a determining, demanding, dictator style of commands that come from his lips. He is even degrading at times. He knows he does not have to sugar coat his words because if any of them are insubordinate or not willing to carry out his or Mistress's orders, they would be killed on the spot. There would be no questions asked, and no one would hold him accountable for doing so because it is expected. Gabe let his mind relax for a moment and think about yesterday morning when he was in bed with Mistress in her arms relaxing after she anally dominated him and used him orally for her pleasure while tugging at the leash attached to his collar around his neck. He feels himself getting aroused at the very thought of it. He feels the blood fill his cock as he stands still in front of everyone exposed for all to see. He doesn't care what anyone of them thinks of him. That is what makes him such an effective leader or second in command in Lucifer's army. Unlike the human side, a demon disobeying him will cost him or her life or the lives of their families. He is not there to build them up. He expects nothing short of everything from them mentally, physically and even emotionally. He doesn't have to bargain to get it. Gabe's mind continues to think about being close to Mistress while feeling her lips on his. He loves feeling her body close to his, skin against skin while feeding on the heat of each other's sweaty, exhausted bodies. She rode him hard and long last night just the way he loves it. All he could think and say from his lips as he thought about being in Mistress's arms is "Mine."

He let the word escape from his mouth out loud.

"Mine what Sir?" one of the demons asked who is in earshot.

Gabe snaps back into reality.

"I was not talking to you, but now you have my attention. Show me your post," Gabe demanded.

Instant regret fills the demon for asking Gabe the question. None of them like to be in the spotlight when it comes to Mistress or Gabe. It was never a good place to be.

Samuel's palms are sweaty. Sweaty palms are something new to him. He never got nervous before a big operation or an arrest. However, this is different. If things don't go right tomorrow, not only will it cost him his life, it will contribute to the possibility of costing the lives of other fighters as well as lives of humanity as a whole. Samuel does not feel like talking or socializing with anyone. He wants to sit and be quiet before the storm comes tomorrow. He lets his mind go blank while he watches the blades of grass sway back and forth with the wind. He prayed earlier with Father Hannigan as well as by himself in the shower earlier. He called his mother to tell her that his friend Larry will drop off her prescription, bread, and milk to her tomorrow morning at 9:00 am time frame.

"Why are you not doing it?" she asked him. "You know I don't like strangers." she reminded him.

"I know Ma, but I have some work to take care of, and I won't be able to do it. You need your medicine. So be nice to him." he pleaded with her.

"I am always nice. What are you trying to say? I'm not nice?" she asked annoyed.

"No Ma, you are always nice. I love you so much. Thank you for everything Ma. Without you, I would have been lost." he said to her in a low voice.

"Samuel, is everything okay? You're scaring me," she said in a broken concerned voice.

"Everything is good Ma. I have to go. I love you." he said to get off the phone.

"I love you too," she replied.

Samuel did not want to prolong the conversation. He would have broken down and cried like a baby with his mother as a release. She always can make him do so in a stressful situation, which always made him feel better afterward. Yes, Ma always makes me feel better he thought to himself as he watches the dancing blades of grass. Always.

Azasar stands on the left side of Mistress as she finishes briefing her first lieutenants. The night air has a calmness to it thought Azasar. It is like the calm before the storm thought Azasar. He knows he cannot afford to make any mistakes. Mistress would not let him live through another one. He looks around the semi-circle of first lieutenants. All have different expressions of emotions on their faces, especially since they heard that the angels are fighting with the humans. If I have to die, I would rather it be done at the hands of the angels and not by Mistress Azasar thought to himself. At least they would show me mercy. Mistress would prolong my agony for her sadistic pleasure for days if not weeks or months. She is the head demon for a reason he thought as heAzasar takes in a long deep slow breath to calm his being. Mistress notices that his breathing pattern has changed.

"Are you still with us Azasar?" she asked in a low tone where not all could hear.

"Yes, Mistress," Azasar answered in kind so that only she and a very close few could hear him as well.

"Good. Let's keep it that way." Mistress ordered.

"Yes Mistress," Azasar said with a broken voice.

Azasar feels like a little child in her presence. He wanted her approval, but not her direct attention because he was not sure what her attention would mean for him at any given time. He wants to please her. He wants to see her look at him with approving eyes again and smile as she did before he made a mess of things with Jordan. There was a time he was in her good grace. There was a time he would frequent her bed too just like Gabe. Now she can't stand to be in the same room with him. Also, he doesn't want to be in the same room with her either out of fear of what could happen. He is going into battle with a high possibility that he might die, which is not too bad after all he thinks to himself. It's better than living in this hell every day with Mistress thought Azasar as he lets his shoulders relax into a state of resolve.

"Do you need anything else, Father?" Felix asked Father Hannigan.

"No thank you, Felix," Father Hannigan answered him.

Felix has been so helpful with making sure everyone has what he or she needs as well as to feel at ease. Father Hannigan says a quick prayer of thanks and blessing for Felix. As Father Hannigan sits on one of the wooden crates that are lined along the outer edge of the field, he says a silent prayer to himself for the battle tomorrow. He prays for the souls that will soon be lost and the injured that will be left behind. He prays that the ones who remain behind still have a lot of fight in them to carry on for future battles. He prays that he would still be by their sides to fight as well. A humble man by nature, Father Hannigan is grateful that God has chosen him to partake in the battle for God and humankind against Satan and his demons from hell. He is sixty-three years old. By the grace of God, he moves around like a man in his thirties. He is still a young man in an old man's body. His mind is as sharp as ever, and he is even more determined to do God's will not only in this life but the next life as well. Father Hannigan stands and starts with the closest person to him. He asks "Do you want to say a quick prayer with me, child?"

"Yes Father." the young timid looking fair complexion short thin girl replied.

We will change things in our favor one prayer at a time thought Father Hannigan as he begins to pray with a bowed head while holding the girl's hands in each of his hands.

"Our Father who art in Heaven. Hallowed be thou name."

As he stands on the side of the good, Jacob, the demon, never felt so at home or so belonged in all his existence. He has been welcomed unconditionally and treated as one of them by all including the angels who follow Michael's orders without question to accept him and treat him as one of their comrades. He will defend their cause and fight to his death if it requires such a sacrifice. He has his selfish reasons as well. Mistress took his wife's and daughter's lives. He wants to take her life in return. He wants to destroy all her hard work and all that she holds dear. Jacob sees Father Hannigan praying with the fighters one by one and even multiple ones at once as well. He starts to wonder if, but before he could finish his thought, Father Hannigan stops in front of him.

"Jacob, I know you don't believe in our God, but I want to pray to God that you stay safe in battle as well. You are a part of our team, a part of our family and by the grace of God you will still be standing tomorrow by our side after the dust settles and our weapons are put away."

Jacob is overcome with emotion as his eyes tear up and one tear rolls down his left cheek. All he could say is "Telsa."

Father Hannigan smiles warmly. He knows who Jacob is talking to.

Alicia looks over across the battlefield. She sees Jacob with the priest praying. She does not judge him or condemn her brother. Instead, she feels love and respect for him for standing up for something that he believes in even if it is standing against his own kind. She knows how he feels about family and especially about Telsa and Fione. Mistress had to see this one coming like a head-on collision Alicia thought to herself. Then again, Mistress has always felt that she is beyond reproach, beyond accountability to anyone except for Lucifer and most importantly beyond being challenged as well as questioned Alicia thought while correcting her thoughts in her process.

She will kill many humans tomorrow, but she will not kill her brother. She would die first at the hands of the humans, angels, Gabe or Mistress. It did not matter. I am with you always brother she said to herself before being interrupted by a very annoying voice.

"Show me your station, Alicia," Gabe ordered with determination on his face. His previous smile that he had at their last meeting was like a ghost that had evaporated leaving no trace of existence. Alicia jumped into action and did as her boss ordered. Please for the love of saneness do not try to have small talk with me today she thought to herself as she presented her station on the sideline. She did not have to worry about that. Today Gabe is all business with his mind on conquering angels to heaven, killing humans and ONE demon.

The night is long and cold. It is not too cold to make sleep unobtainable. No, the temperature is not the reason that both sides are finding it hard to sleep tonight. Fear, apprehension, uncertainty, adrenaline, praying, thoughts of family and mortality are just a few catalysts that are keeping sleeping at bay tonight. Even though it feels like time is going very slow tonight, morning is coming at the speed of a runaway train while war, as well as mortality, is just beyond the horizon at noon.

The multi-billionaire sits on the sideline in attire that he would have never picked out himself. Terrance mindset, as well as his approach to life in general, have now changed drastically over the past few months since he met Michael, Auroa and the other fighters. He is clearly not the man he used to be before he was approached by Michael to join in the fight against the demons on God's behalf as well as humankind's behalf. Three nights ago he had an unexpected as well as an unwelcomed visit from Daisy. She expected to find him pining over her and distraught over not being with her. On the contrary, he was happy she was not in his life anymore. He never thought he would feel that way because he used to believe in the past that he loved her more than life itself. He thought he loved her more than his money, family, business, church, friends and even himself. When he opened the door, he was very disappointed to see her standing on the other side smiling her smile that used to melt him down into his shoes in the past.

So many countless days and night she used that smile to manipulate him into getting her way. When he saw her, he felt nothing but contempt. His thoughts drifted back to the conversation that night.

"Hello, Terrance," Daisy said in her seductive voice through a beautiful smile that would have brought Terrance to his knees in the past. Terrance stood in the doorway blocking her entrance while not inviting her in.

"Daisy, what are you doing here?" Terrance asked in a stern voice. Daisy was taken back a little with his demeanor towards her. It was clear to the both of them that she expected to be received by him in an entirely different way.

Finally, she spoke after a moment of disbelief. "Aren't you going to invite me inside?" she asked through lips that were no longer smiling.

"No Daisy. There is no reason for you to be here, no reason for us to talk and there is no reason we should waste our time with each other anymore." Terrance said to her as he closed the door in front of her while she was still standing on the porch in disbelief. Terrance walked silently back upstairs to his room. He felt nothing for her. All he felt inside was closure. Then the thought of Auroa drifted into his mind as he made it to his room. A smile formed on his face as his body and mind filled with welcomed happiness. It was clear to him that his affection for Daisy had died and was now replaced by his affection and desire for Auroa.

"Do you have everything you need?" Uriel asked Terrance interrupting his warm thoughts of Auroa while bringing his mind back to the present.

"Yes, yes I have everything I need and more Uriel," he answered with a smile forming on his face as he looks down the sideline of the battlefield in the direction of Auroa. Michael heard his response and followed his line of sight to Auroa. Michael's fists tighten slightly for a little second. Michael forced himself to relax, turn and walk away. Yeah, I got it bad Michael thought as he walks toward other fighters on the sideline.

Edward sits in a chair that is designated for him on the sideline of the battlefield near Mistress's elevated chair. He had just finished walking along the sideline checking on every soldier and making sure they had their head in the battle that will be upon them in a matter of minutes. Even though he is pure evil and very sadistic, he is also more in tune with the feelings of others, unlike Mistress and Gabe. He picks up and uses the feelings of others to his advantage. In this case, he uses his ability to calm the demon fighters while still motivating them to fight to the death if need be. Edward's mind relaxes and goes into a state of calmness as he looks over at the other side of the field with the eyesight of a hawk. He looks at the faces of old, middle-aged and young adults standing on the sideline. Some even look like children, which is not the case. Children are not allowed to fight in the battles. They will play a role in other ways in the future.

As his gaze travels along the sideline, his eyes catch its first glimpse of Auroa. His body becomes alert instantly, and his eyes become more focused as he continues to look at her. She aroused his being in a way that he hasn't felt in a hundred years. Her fair skin and her full round face make him want to reach out and touch her skin. He can tell that she is a full figured woman, which he loves and adores about a woman. One should always have something to hold on to as well as cushion him when torturing her he thought with a smile forming on his face.

"Edward, how is the sideline holding up?" his trance was interrupted by Mistress asking a question.

"It's holding up well Ma'am. The sideline is solid," he replied after being snapped back into reality by Mistress's voice and question.

"Good. Let's keep it that way," she said to him.

"Yes Ma'am," Edward replied.

"By the way she is not for you. Stay away from her. She is off limits to all demons. Stay away from Auroa. Do I make myself clear?" Mistress asked while warning and ordering at the same time.

She saw him gazing and lusting at Auroa. She knows Edward way too well to know that the look in his eyes is one that would and could cost her the war if he goes to visit her or try to interact with her in any form or fashion. Instantly she knows that Edward is fixated on Auroa. Auroa is in his mind. I will be damned if I let his lustful ways jeopardize all I have worked for and hope to accomplish Mistress thought to as her gaze grows more intent on Edward.

"Yes Ma'am, very clear," he replied.

"If you look like you are disobeying me, it will cost you your life immediately. No questions will be asked. I will kill you." Mistress warned.

"Yes, Ma'am. I understand and will obey." Edward said submissively.

Dammit, all to hell he thought. I just have to lust from afar for now, yes, for now, he thought as he turns away to prevent himself from looking at Auroa again. Mistress watches him for a moment with a suspicious eye and then she turns her attention to another matter. After all, she has to be on top of everything in the bigger picture of it all.

After she finished making her rounds on her side of the battlefield, Mistress walks slowly and gracefully in her high heel black leather boots over to her elevated throne-like chair in the middle of the sideline on her side of the field. She effortlessly climbs the six steps up to her platform where her chair is located. Her formfitting purple outfit enhances her sexuality as her hips sway back and forth as she climbs the steps. She turns and stands for a while in front of her chair at the top of the platform. She surveys the battlefield as a whole. She pays close attention to her sideline while taking in every detail and looking for weaknesses. She zeros in on conversations that were quite a distance away to determine the mindset of her fighters. Once she is finished checking out her side of the battlefield, she checks out her opponent's sideline. Even though she cannot zero in on their conversations due to the protocols that are in place, she did pay attention to their body languages and facial expressions. That alone told her a lot about them. They are scared but full of determination. They appear to be ready to fight to the death. She sees the angels, whom she could not read at all. Then she sees Jacob standing with a priest.

"A priest Jacob. Really. I mean really." she said aloud between clutched teeth.

She moves her eyes and attention away from him. She could not let her anger of him get in the way of seeing the big picture. She has to remain focused. It's not about him. There is a bigger picture she thinks to herself. She won't deter or falters in her determination to do what needs to be done to win. Mistress sits down very slowly in her chair. Two servants rush to her side to make her comfortable. She waves them away with her hands. They retreat immediately and sit five feet away from her one on each side of her chair to wait for a time when they would be needed. Mistress knows her orders. Lucifer came to her last night. He gave her specific instructions that ended with one word, WIN! Then he brutally beat and raped her over and over and over again for his pleasure. A slight smile forms on her face. Yes, I have been taught by the best she thought to herself.

Azasar fuckups really put a monkey wrench into my plans thought Mistress. Mistress can see glimpses of the future. She has foreseen that Jordan will play a major part in which side will win the overall war to rule on Earth. Now that the battles are about to begin, Mistress cannot touch her. Mistress does not know the details about what role Jordan will play or for what side Jordan will end up playing for, but without Jordan, the overall winner will not win in the end. If Azasar had killed her before the start of the war, it would not be a chance that Jordan would help the other side win. However, Jordan could play a role in helping the demon side to win as well, but Mistress was not willing to take a fifty-fifty chance gamble that it could go either way. Therefore, she sent Azasar out to kill Jordan before she could influence things either way. Mistress did not know what Jordan looked like or her actual name at the time. Mistress only saw Jordan's house that she lived in. Therefore, Azasar had to figure out which adult was the first lieutenant in Jordan's house. Fucking Azasar she thought as she takes a deep breath to calm herself. Mistress made a conscientious effort to push Azasar and his major fuckup out of her mind. She could not afford to let anything or anyone cloud her judgment during battle. She lets her muscles relax while she releases her tight grip on the arms of her chair. She looks over to her slaves and beckons for them to come. She pats her shoulder for one and points at her feet for the other. They assume the positions and start to get her ready for a massage of her shoulders, neck, arms, legs, and feet. Mistress takes a deep breath and closes her eyes while she let them serve her.

The morning seems to last a lifetime. Both sides are eager to start and yet dreading the losses and injuries that will occur soon enough. The first lieutenants on both sides did their last rounds to ensure everything and everyone are in place. Also, they made sure that the fighters were in the mindset of putting up a fight of a lifetime that would win not only battles but wars. Mistress does her rounds as well as talks to every demon under her command. Even though they are all nervous, they want to please her and win for her. They want to be in her good grace. They all are willing to fight to the death if that is what is needed to please Mistress and help her to win the battle. Mistress is proud of every one of them, even Azasar at this moment. He is eager to please her as well. Even though he knows his days are numbered, he will do everything to the best of his ability to please Mistress and make all her wishes a reality. The essence of a true servant Mistress thought to herself as she walks past him and glances momentarily in his direction. She nods her head slightly to acknowledge his presence. Azasar gasps from the surprise of receiving an acknowledgment from her. Tears well up in his eyes. Even though she has caused him so much pain and anguish, Azasar still loves and serves her with all of his being and existence. He longs for the day when she would look at him with approving eyes and smiles.

Gregory's mind is focused and intent on accomplishing the events of the day. He has trained very hard for this privilege to fight on behalf of God and humankind. What an honor he thought as he laced up his right boot a third, and in his mind, vowed to be a final time. His thoughts drifted to his mother who he left crying earlier yesterday morning in her doorway. She has hidden her fears and feelings very well over the past few months. She has honestly been his rock. However, the possibility that she could be seeing him alive for the last time was too overwhelming for her during their final hug goodbye yesterday morning. She started to cry uncontrollably while she kept saying "I'm sorry. I'm sorry. I love you. I'm sorry. I love you."

"You never have to apologize to me for loving me Mom." Gregory consoled her.

After an extended period of silent embrace, he released her and said "I'll see you tomorrow. I love you."

"I love you too," she replied through tears.

Gregory picked up his bag and looked into his Mother's eyes one last time before turning and walking at a fast pace off the porch and out the driveway. He did not turn to look back at her. He did not want her to see the tears streaming silently down his face. He did not want her to worry more than she already was or see him cry.

He took a deep breath of the morning air and exhaled it slowly while he focused on the thought that he had a plane to catch.

Now that he is finally on the battlefield waiting what seems like a lifetime, he feels as though he is seeing things and people in slow motion. It is so incredulous. However, he knows it's real and believes in the inevitability of battle. He is ready to give all he has to win or die with honor trying.

"Would you like to say a small prayer with me, my son?" Father Hannigan asked interrupting his train of thought.

"Yes, Father," Gregory replied as he grasps Father Hannigan's hand and bows his head.

The air seems thick to T'Ariel. The outfit feels light even though it looks cumbersome on her small frame. Her long brown hair blows in the wind. This just won't do she thought as she gathers it to the back of her head. I should have brought a brush she thought as she tries to hold onto her thick hair with one hand while trying to gather up the loose strands flying in the wind.

"Let me help you T'Ariel." offers one of the female fighters.

"Thanks, please do," T'Ariel replied.

The female fighter pulls her thick wavy brown hair back and braids it nice and neatly. She even has a tie to put on the end of it as well.

"Thank you so much," T'Ariel said to the young lady.

"No problem," she replied with a broad smile while she turns and walks back to her station on the sideline.

T'Ariel did not have anyone to say goodbye to this morning. No family is waiting for her to return from battle. She is an orphan. She has been on her own since she turned eighteen. She had been in and out of foster homes because her mother and father were deemed unfit to care for her since she was five years old. Apparently, their drug habit was more important than her. She has had a hard life growing up. Surprisingly she remained positive and optimistic. It was by the grace of God. She found the Lord early in her young life. He was and still is her beacon of hope and in her mind her knight in shining armor.

I do this for you my Lord she thought as she sits down on the sideline. She glances over at Gregory praying with Father Hannigan and smiles. She never felt so peaceful and hopeful as she does at this very moment. She lets her mind wander as her smile broaden while she thinks of the possibilities of what could be with Gregory.

Claudia is more focused and determined than ever to make a name for herself on the battlefield. Her ambition is spilling over in her obsessive compulsion in checking to make sure everything is in place, right and ready for battle. She informs the ones below her that she will tolerate no fuckups or hiccups. They know to take her very gravely serious. For it could cost them their lives if they don't. Claudia walks over and gives Gabe a report on her section of the fighters. She always wants to please Gabe. He is her idol and mentor. Gabe took her under his wing when he saw a lot of him in her when he was her age thousands of years ago. He mentored and molded her into a perfect use to be younger version of him. They have a tight bond like father and daughter. She is his masterpiece. After briefing Gabe, Claudia goes back to her section of the sideline and sits in her designated chair. She takes a moment to steady herself, clear her mind and relax before the storm of battle. All of her soldiers know not to disturb her at this moment unless it is critical and can't wait. Claudia lets her mind think about something that would help her to relax. She thinks about her next bully victim that she would take great pleasure in bullying, torturing, driving mad and ultimately killing her or him in the end. A beautiful, peaceful smile forms on her face from sheer mental pleasure.

Mistress makes one last round with her fighters. Mistress last stop before she returns to her elevated chair is to stand beside Gabe at the center of the sideline of the field. They do not speak. They silently stand next to each other and enjoy the closeness of each other for a moment. No words are needed. Their silent bond speaks volumes between the two of them. Mistress and Gabe turn and look at each other in silence for a moment. She smiles slightly while Gabe smiles broadly. Slowly she breaks their gaze and turns to walk away. She climbs the steps to her chair and slowly sits down. Once she is seated, she takes a deep breath and exhales slowly.

"Soon, very soon," she said aloud to herself as she rested her head back against the chair.

Mistress sits in her chair calmly as her servants attend her. She does not even acknowledge her daughter at her left side. It is always custom for her daughter to stand at her left hand side when they both are together in a place or room. It means that if something should happen to Mistress, Patricia is supposed to move to the right and assume power because she is the next in command. Gabe would then be Patricia's right-hand man. When Mistress is not present, Patricia is understood even by Gabe that she has the reign of power. Even though she is young in demon age, Patricia is almost as powerful as Mistress. However, Patricia is more even keel and more level-headed at times than Mistress. Also, she can be more evil than Mistress at times as well. After all, Patricia is the daughter of Lucifer and Mistress. She is more like her father than her mother in more ways than one and especially in the ways that count the most. Her power will grow a thousand folds more powerful than Mistress when she turns three hundred years old in two years. Patricia is content at the moment at Mistress's left side. One day she will take her place as the leader by force if not given to her by the will of Mistress. When the time comes, not only will Patricia's power demand her to ascend to power, but Lucifer himself would demand that his daughter ascend as well.

Auroa is very nervous about the centerfield meeting she will soon have with Mistress at noon. Michael senses her uneasiness. He walks over to her and sits beside her. At first, Michael waits for her to say something to him. After an extended period, he realizes that she is not going to speak and volunteer what is on her mind.

"Auroa are you nervous about meeting Mistress in the middle of the field at noon?" he asked in a low soft voice that sounded more like music than spoken words.

"Yes," she answered in a low soft voice that could barely be heard.

"Don't be. Look at me Auroa." Michael said.

She slowly raises her gaze to meet his.

"Don't be. God has chosen you. He believes in you. I believe in you. Everyone around you believes in you. Now I want and need you to believe in you." Michael reassured her.

As he spoke, she felt all her anxiety and nervousness melt away. Is this what it means and feels like to have an angel on your shoulder or in your corner Auroa thought to herself. Michael could see her shoulders, body, and face relax.

"Now let's go and talk to everyone to let them know that we believe in them too," he said standing up and holding out his hand to her.

Auroa smiles while taking his hand and standing up by his side. They walked all morning together talking to every fighter on the sideline, humans, angels and demon alike.

All the fighters on both sides are dressed in formfitting clothes with body armor or metal mesh over their clothing as well as helmets for head protection. All forms of knives, bows, axes, ball and chains, and any non-gun type of weapons are held in the hands of the fighters on the sidelines. Auros's and Mistress's high chairs are on opposite sidelines facing each other. Mistress and Auroa both have two guards standing post near their chairs for protection. Mistress has demons for her protection while Auroa has angels for hers.

Michael turns to Auroa and says "It's time."

Auroa takes a deep breath and starts to walk out towards the middle of the field. Mistress begins to descend her steps from her chair slowly gracefully and walks towards the middle of the field to meet Auroa for the first time. She is beautiful Auroa thought as she lays eyes on Mistress for the first time. Tall and beautiful. Her voluptuous body is alluring and very inviting. However, there is something that is foreboding about her that makes Auroa want to turn and run in the other direction as well. Something that makes Auroa feel that she is in grave danger even though she knows Mistress can't touch her without forfeiting winning the overall war.

She is so fragile Mistress thought as she locks her gaze on Auroa. I could easily snatch the life out of her. Bring her to her knees effortlessly Mistress thought to as she walks towards Auroa. Mistress takes a deep breath to control her desires and impulses to annihilate not only Auroa's existence, but all who follow her as well. Mistress has the power to kill them all with the wave of her hand, save the angels. However, protocol prohibits her from doing so. Protocols, protocols, damn protocols Mistress chimed in her mind. As she approaches Auroa, she smiles a broad smile revealing perfectly straight white teeth. Beautiful Auroa thought to herself, but she did not return the smile.

"So you are the human leader." Mistress stated instead of asking.

"So you are the Demon Mistress." Auroa retorted.

Mistress likes her for some reason in a small way. The way Auroa holds her gaze and carries herself as she stands in front of

Mistress gives her a sense of confidence which Mistress instantly respects.

"I'm Mistress." Mistress introduced herself and held out her hand to Auroa.

"I am Auroa." Auroa reaches out and shakes Mistress's hand with a firm grip while maintaining eye contact.

Mistress's smile broadens as their hands touch. Auroa returns the smile in kind. They release their hand embrace slowly.

"We will meet again and again and again Auroa." Mistress said as they both took a step backward from each other.

"I look forward to it," Auroa replied.

"Yes, it will be my pleasure as well." Mistress replied as they both turned and walked back to their respective sideline.

Once Mistress and Auroa returned to their side and seated themselves in their chairs with their guards protecting them, Mistress's first lieutenants take charge of Mistress's front line while the angels take charge of Auroa's frontline. Each side bellowed out orders and words of motivation. Gabe and Michael hold up their right hands and motion for their fighters to go forward. Both sides yell out as they hold up their weapons of choice and run out towards the middle of the field. The demons are stronger, faster and heal from minor cuts and bruises immediately while the humans are determined and relentless at winning this battle. The training and sheer determination that the humans have are a good combination that would give them an edge where it counts the most on the battlefield.

The humans are working in synch with the angels. Quickly the demons realize that this is not going to be as easy of a battle as some had thought it would be. Auroa watches from the sideline as Michael wield his sword. It always hit its mark quickly, decisively and effectively. His speed is unbelievable. Auroa thought that she would not be able to stand to look at all the fighting, the killing, the blood, and gruesomeness of the battle, but it's quite the opposite. She cannot take her eyes off the field in part because of her concern for the welfare of all the fighters under her as well as her desire to be informed of what is unfolding on the battlefield.

As many demons become airborne on the field, the angels become airborne as well to meet them in midair to smite them down to the ground. Michael twirls and changes his positions remarkably well in midair to cut off two heads of demons who flank him in the air. He is not only an excellent leader and trainer but a formidable fighter and soldier as well.

T'Ariel is holding her own remarkably well considering her size and the seemingly big outfit she is wearing. Her moves look like a female version of Michael without being airborne or extremely quick. One demon looks over at her thinking she would be an easy kill. T'Ariel easily ducks down out of the way as the demon cut through the air with his sword towards her head. While still in the bending position, T'Ariel thrust her sword into the heart of the demon host body hitting its mark. Without hesitation, she pulls her sword out and cuts off the demon's head. There was no time to relish in her win this time. She continues to fight as if she was born to do so. Her tiny body is moving smoothly through the moving collage of fighters on the battlefield.

Gregory wields his sword as if it is an extension of his body. At one point he kneels down and picks up a second sword as two demons attack him at once. He kills one demon in front of him with one sword in one hand while wielding his sword in his other hand to his back to block a sword blow from the other demon. He quickly turns to face his opponent. The demon is stronger than Gregory. He strikes swords with Gregory in midair which sends Gregory backward to the ground. Gregory reaches back with his free hand to block his body from falling entirely to the ground. Gregory continues to fight in his semi-kneeling position. He manages to cut the demon's leg deeply with one of his blows. It is just the opportunity that Gregory needs to have a chance to reposition his body to a standing position. He turns around, and with all his might, he swings his sword to the midsection of the demon almost cutting it in half. He uses one foot to push the demon off his sword. The demon's host body falls lifeless to the ground. Gregory continues to fight without skipping a beat.

Mistress glances across the field at an unnatural speed that enables her to take in all the fighting almost at once. She has no expression on her face until she sees an angel approach Gabe who had fallen to his knees as the might of the angel's blade met his. Naturally, the angel is stronger and more powerful than him. The blow from the angel knocked him backward fifteen feet while knocking the breath out of him and bringing him to his knees. Mistress's face is stricken with fear and pain as she watches helplessly as her most trusted companion is about to die. Everything seems to move in slow motion as the angel takes eight long strides towards him while raising his sword above his head in a downward stabbing stance to deal the final blow of death to Gabe. Without warning and unexpectedly, Azasar jumps in front of Gabe and takes the strike of the sword up to the hilt in his right chest. It gives Gabe a chance to recover and flee imminent danger. Instantly in Mistress's eyes, Azasar has redeemed himself back up to third in command. She not only forgives all he has done in the past, she feels protective of him as well. She wants to run out and protect him, heal him and personally thank him, but protocol prohibits her from doing so. Her and Auroa are not allowed on the battlefield for any of the battles except for the last battle to be fought in the war. They can participate in the final battle as well as be tempted and killed in action. That is why the presence of the angels are so disturbing to Mistress. They can kill her, but she has no power to destroy them.

Azasar holds the angel's blade to his body to give Gabe a chance to recover and flee to another area on the battlefield. The angel pulls his sword from Azasar effortlessly. When he looks for Gabe, he is already gone. Without skipping a beat, the angel goes on to strike down other multiple demons that are close to him. Azasar falls to the ground. He is not dead yet, but he feels that life is slowly draining out of him. There are five minutes left to fight on the battlefield. The first fifty-nine minutes seemed like a lifetime not only to the fighters but to Mistress and Auroa as well.

Claudia's speed is awe-inspiring as she wields her sword and ax wounding and killing humans without remorse or sympathy. Most she only strikes once, but a few carefully chosen ones she strikes multiple times to ensure they are dead. Those are the humans who put up the most challenging fight towards her. Claudia makes her way towards T'Ariel who is unaware that Claudia is approaching her from behind. As Claudia grows near she raises her sword to deal the deathblow to T'Ariel, it is met in midair by Gregory's sword. T'Ariel turns around because of the loud metal clash behind her. She stands wide-eyed and is semi-shocked as she sees the swords inches away from her head.

"Snap out of it T!" Gregory yells out.

T'Ariel snaps out of her shocked trans and starts to help Gregory fight Claudia. Even though there are two of them, they are still no match for Claudia. Raphael sees the two young fighters struggling. He rushes to their aid just in time. Claudia feels fear for the first time on the battlefield as the Archangel who is faster and stronger than she takes over the fight. He easily and quickly delivers a blow that cuts off her right hand holding her sword. She tries to wield the ax, and her left arm that is holding her ax falls to the ground as well. She is completely defenseless. Raphael for some reason did not cut off her head. Instead, he mortally wounds her and stabs her in the chest up to his sword's hilt. He removes his sword from her chest like a hot knife exits warm butter. Her body falls to the ground as she is trying desperately to cling to life until the end of the battle.

For the first time, Auroa stands on her feet when she sees four demons attack an angel dressed in all white. She sees his white outfit turn red with multiple cuts. Even though the demons cannot kill the angel, they can kill the body that the angel occupies. As one of the demons deals the final death blow to the body by cutting off the head, a bright blinding light appears around the angel's host body that instantly incinerate the demons that are near it in a five-foot radius. It did not affect the humans. The angel left the body to find another host to occupy or to return to heaven. Michael and all the other angels instantly know and feel what is going on with the displaced angel on the battlefield. It only intensifies their fighting.

Jacob saw what happened to the other demons close to the angel when it's host body was destroyed. He makes a mental note not to stand too close to an angel on the battlefield. It worried him a little as well because one cannot be conscientious of everyone's place on the battlefield. Terrance fights close to Jacob during the battle. At times they would team up to fight against one or two demons together. Jacob sees Alicia, and he sees Terrance notice her as well. He makes his way to Terrance.

"Please don't touch that one Terrance. It is my sister," he asked with a pleading look on his face.

Alicia heard him ask Terrance not to touch her. She purposely made her way in the opposite direction away from them on the battlefield without making it obvious. She did not want the other demons or Mistress to pick up on what she was doing.

Jordan is at her best in her familiar element of fighting a good fight. As one demon falls as a result of her sword or one on one combat, she does not hesitate to move on quickly to deal a swift blow to the next demon close by. It is easy to determine demons from humans and angels fighters. Demons fighters wear all black helmets while human fighters wear white helmets. The angels and Jacob do not wear a helmet at all. Jordan's training in the CIA is finally being put to good use.

Edward is in the lap of luxury. He loves the battle, the chaos, the torture, inflicting pain, and most of all killing humans. He purposely cut off arms and legs to leave the humans dying an agonizing death as blood drains from their bodies. Even in the midst of battle, the image of Auroa goes through his mind. He smiles as he thinks to himself maybe I won't listen to you this time Mistress. With his mind's revelation of freedom from Mistress's orders, he changes his fighting tactics and inflicts stomach wounds to multiple humans nearby as a celebration of being liberated from the control of Mistress in his mind. A liberation that may cost him his life, but that does not deter him, not even a little bit.

Samuel has tunnel vision as he has always been in getting a job done. He is surprised that he is not getting tired. His adrenalin keeps him strong, alert and in constant motion through what seemed like an unlimited supply of energy. Samuel glances over just in time to see Father Hannigan get stabbed in the back by one of the demons while he was busy fighting another demon in front of him.

Samuel yells out "NO!" as he runs towards Father Hannigan. Father Hannigan drops his sword and falls to his knees. Samuel runs over with his sword drawn back over his head. With one decisive blow, he cuts off the head of the demon who stabbed Father Hannigan in the back. Samuel does not have time to stop and talk to the Father safely. Therefore, he stands next to him to protect him by fighting off any future demon attacks that are bound to happen if he was not there. At the end of the battle, all who have not lost their lives completely will be healed and made whole to fight in another battle. The dead will remain dead even though the angels and Mistress have the power to revive them.

"Hold on Father!" Samuel yelled out while striking a demon in the face with the helve of his sword.

Both Mistress and Auroa are standing on their feet while the last few seconds of the battle comes to an end. A bright almost blinding light appears over the middle of the field. Everyone instantly stops fighting. It was hard to look up at the bright light. All the living are instantly healed and made whole while the dead remain lying still and lifeless on the field. Samuel turns to Father Hannigan and sees him standing effortlessly to his feet. Mistress breathe a sigh of relief as well when she sees Azasar rise to his feet. Each fighter goes back to their perspective side of the field. Michael locks eyes with Auroa as he exits the field. If he didn't know better, he would swear that she aged years since he last saw her.

Gabe and Azasar walk off the field together. Mistress looks at Azasar and gives him an approving nod. Azasar feels as though he is standing ten feet tall. She is looking at him with approving eyes. He would have taken ten or more swords to the chest for this moment. However, he is glad that he did not have to. One is truly enough he thought to himself.

Once everyone is on their sideline, they all look back at the bloody body filled battlefield. So many are lost thought Auroa, so many. Mistress expectation was met and exceeded by her fighters. She is very pleased, very pleased indeed. The bright light lingers in the middle of the field for a few moments longer and then drifts over to the human side of the field. They all let out a loud cheer. They won the battle at a great cost. So many lay dead on the ground. Before the healing, so many were near death. Mistress's face grows stern, but she did not lose control. She gracefully nods in the direction of Auroa who returns the nod as well.

Michael looks up at Auroa and says "This has been a day of days."

His broad, handsome, happy smile instantly lifts Auroa to an even higher level mentally and emotionally than she already is because of the win.

"Yes Michael a day of days," she replied through her happy smile as well.

There will be a time to fight again, but not today. There will be a time to die again, but not today. There will be a time for sorrow and pain, but not today. Not today.

Prelude to the Next Novel

"What is your will Father?" Xzavia asked Lucifer while kneeling before him.

"My son, my firstborn, the demons have lost the first major battle against the humans. I am greatly disappointed in Mistress, to say the least. She will feel my wrath soon enough. However, I have a special task at hand for you. There is a special relic that is one of the most powerful relics of them all. It is not an object parse. It consists of eight children who are all the age of ten. These are not ordinary children. Each of them has a special ability. An ability that can be used for good or evil. Whoever captures a child, controls his or her ability. In order to claim the relic as a whole for a specific side, five of the children must be claimed by one side. Once five children are captured by one side, the other three children's abilities will be lost to the five who are captured together. The three remaining children become useless ordinary children. I want you to take your two sisters and three brothers and walk the Earth. Bring me no less than five children Xzavia, no less. You are free to reign holy hell on all you encounter except for Mistress. For she is mine, and my idea of hell is hers." Lucifer commanded his son.

"Your will is already done Father," he replied.

Xzavia gets up and walks quickly out of his Father's chamber. The air is thick and hot just like Xzavia loves it. The sounds of pain, torture and agonizing cries of hell are his lullabies. Earth will not have such beautiful music Xzavia thought as he walks through the dimmed lighted large tunnel towards his brothers' and sisters' chambers. I guess my brothers, sisters and I will have to make our own music he thought as a wicked smile form on his face as he knocks on his sister's, Chastine, chamber door.

About the Author

Lillie Carr

Desolation

Lillie Carr is a single mother of now two grown young men who are two of the greatest people she has ever known. She was born and raised in Brunswick, Georgia until the day she left at the age of nineteen to join the United States Navy, of which she served almost eight years in. After the Navy, she found herself called to serve others again in nursing, which she continues to this day for over twenty years. Between being a mother, nursing and finding herself again after a divorce of a seventeen and a half years marriage, she wrote Desolation and started on the sequel to Desolation as well. She owes all that she is and will become to the Lord Thy Savior Jesus Christ who not only guides her steps in life but guides her imagination and pen as well.

Made in United States
Orlando, FL
28 April 2022

17278627R00146